A MESSAGE FROM CHICKEN HOUSE

Of course it's not safe in that secret world beyond the postal portal – especially when there are villainous plans afoot – but Emily goes anyway. Luckily her hedgehog and headstrong humour don't (quite) put off her friends. Just as well: she needs them! What happens next is all wonderful mayhem and madcap adventures. My favourite bits are Emily's attempts to transform into her animal Pooka selves, and her ghostly ghastly ghûl best friend, long-suffering junior policeman Tarkus. Talented authors Ben and Laura are masters of a universe like no other!

BARRY CUNNINGHAM
Publisher
Chicken House

THE
MIDNIGHT
HOWL

BENJAMIN READ & LAURA TRINDER

2 PALMER STREET, FROME, SOMERSET BA11 1DS

Story: Trindles & Read
Words: Read

Text © Read Books Ltd 2020
Interior illustrations © Laura Trinder 2020
Cover illustration © Hannah Peck 2020

First published in Great Britain in 2020
Chicken House
2 Palmer Street
Frome, Somerset BA11 1DS
United Kingdom
www.chickenhousebooks.com

Cover and interior design by Steve Wells
Cover illustration by Hannah Peck
Interior illustrations by Laura Trinder
Typeset by Dorchester Typesetting Group Ltd
Printed and bound in Great Britain by CPI Group (UK) Ltd, Croydon CR0 4YY

The paper used in this Chicken House book is made
from wood grown in sustainable forests.

1 3 5 7 9 10 8 6 4 2

British Library Cataloguing in Publication data available.

PB ISBN 978-1-912626-87-8
eISBN 978-1-913322-21-2

For my wonderful, ever-supportive mum and dad.
(Also, see! I told you letting me stay inside in the warm and
read books about dragons would pay off eventually.)
– BR

For my favourite brother, James.
– LT

'We have heard the chimes at midnight, Master Shallow.'

– WILLIAM SHAKESPEARE

Henry IV Part 2

Act III, Scene II

CHAPTER 1

Emily really hadn't ever expected to be a sister. As an only child, she'd often wondered what it would be like, but had never, at her advanced age, thought it would happen. So even now, many months after the first shocking announcement from her mum and dad that they were, y'know, totally preggers, the whole idea still confuzzled her. When she had nothing better to do she would pick away at it like a satisfyingly crusty scab. Like right now, in fact, during a boring half-term, as she loitered untidily outside her dad's potting shed, watching him elbow deep in stinky compost inside.

'It's just weird. I mean, like, how are you having a baby?'

Emily's dad shifted awkwardly from foot to foot at his potting bench.

'Well, I suppose it's time we had that conversation . . . erm, well when two people love each other very much—'

'NOOOOOOO! ABSOLUTELY NOT. EVER!' screeched Emily.

Emily's dad looked relieved despite the damage to his hearing.

'I meant, how *now*?' said Emily. 'I mean, you're really old.'

'Charming,' said her dad. 'Well, after what happened last year, it made us think about what was important, I suppose.'

With typical dad understatement, he was referring to the mayhem that occurred after a mysterious midnight letter led to him and her mum being kidnapped, and Emily stumbling into the magical London of the Midnight Hour, a pocket dimension frozen in Victorian times that contained the last remnants of magic in the world (and all the monsters). It had been a pretty intense week.

'. . . and this was a happy accident.' He'd still been talking while she was thinking of moon-silvered streets, and being chased by were-bears and vampires. He paused and studied her more closely.

'You do think it's happy too, I hope? You can tell me, you know, if you're worried about any of it.'

Emily shook her head.

'No, it's fine. I'm happy. It's just . . . a lot.' She scrunched her nose up as she thought about it. 'I kind of thought finding out I was a magic pony was the oddest thing that was going to happen for a while, is all.'

'You are not a p—'

'I know, I know. I'm Pooka, it's a proud heritage.'

'I was going to say you're only half magic pony, but yeah, that too.'

'Dad!'

He grinned.

One of the weirdest things about the adventure that had knocked her whole life sideways was finding out her up-to-now totally normal (well, apart from her mum) parents were secretly part of the Midnight Hour them-selves. Her dad was a magic postman and her mum was a Librarian (which was like being a secret agent). The very weirdest thing, of course, was discovering she was a bit magic herself. She had magic pony— *Pooka* heritage from her mum's clan and could transform into a hare and do other freaky stuff, although only, to her disappointment, inside the Midnight Hour, because that's where all the magic was nowadays.

Not that she was getting to go into the Hour at all now, of course.

'Sure you're okay?' He went to touch her shoulder then

stopped as she gazed in horror at his composty hand. 'You don't normally loiter around the shed unless you want something.'

This was true. Emily was of the opinion that the shed smelt funny. She suspected her dad kept it that way so he could have quiet time in there.

'I'm just all . . .' She kicked at the pots in frustration and her dad winced. 'I miss going into the Hour with Mum is all.'

'Ahhh,' he said.

'It was great. We were doing loads of shape-changing practice and I nearly managed the hound. Well,' she paused, 'nearly nearly, and then all the stupid baby stuff happened and now she won't go in anymore and I really miss it . . . and her.'

She blurted the last bit out and hadn't known she was going to say it. That, of course, happened a lot, but normally only when she was angry.

'Ahhh,' her dad said again, in a different tone. He grabbed a rag to wipe his hands on.

'I mean, we weren't even rowing then. Well, much, and now she's a bonkers person again,' said Emily.

'It *was* much more peaceful for a while,' her dad mused. 'It was like a little holiday by the sea.'

'Dad!'

He held a still-grimy hand up to calm her. 'You

understand there's a good reason why she can't, don't you? Pookas can't—'

'Change when they're pregnant,' she finished for him, 'I know. In case of . . .' She gave herself donkey ears with her fingers, and stuck her front teeth right out. According to her mum, Auntie Lavell got stuck as a horse while pregnant once, and little cousin Artie had always been a bit . . . pony ever since. Her dad's lips twitched as he tried not to smile.

'Yes, and there are also serious safety concerns about you going in alone.' He was frowning again. 'You upset some very nasty people, you know.'

She couldn't deny that. She had faced off with the Nocturne, one of the great Older Powers, and defeated her by accidentally blowing her up using a necklace of cursed coins. Emily stared at her trainers. It was hopeless, she was never going to get back in.

'However, in a bid to regain the sanctity of my shed,' said her dad, 'I have already given this a lot of thought, and spoken at length with your mother. Sometimes she even listened.' He shook his head. 'We've decided that while you're on holidays, with appropriate supervision and strict boundaries, it might be okay for you to go back in—'

Before he could finish she jump-hugged him, compost hands or not.

'Yay!' She squeezed him, then paused and glared up. 'Next time, start with that!'

The enthusiastic squishing had restricted his breathing but didn't stop his safety speech.

'*Strict* boundaries. You'd come in with me to work, practise nearby, then we'd leave together. Also your mother has a *major* lecture to deliver before you get to go anywhere.' He fuzzled her hair with his grubby hands, but she was prepared to forgive him under the circumstances. 'Go and see her, she's in the studio.'

'Thanks, Dad!' She skipped at high speed up the garden.

'Mind my pots! Oh, never mind . . .'

It wasn't a proper studio. It was a garage with too much art in to fit a car anymore. Emily had to squeeze down the corridor past metalwork sculptures, plaster hangings and a stack of other piled-up art just to reach the door. Her mum, Maeve, was always busy with her sculpture, but she'd gone mad(der) making things since the pregnancy. Their whole house was becoming a gallery. She'd even started painting again, and apparently she 'hadn't done that since the 1800s'. Emily's mum could say things like that because it turned out she was a magic Pooka person who, until she'd left the Midnight Hour, had been frozen in time since 1859. This was before TV, or cars, or even – *shudder* – indoor loos. Finding out her mum was a magic shape-changing Irish woman in exile from another time had been a shock, but it also answered a lot of questions about why she was so odd.

Her mum was sat at the workbench. Maeve was as pocket-sized as ever, with her trademark big black boots on, but her faded Metallica T-shirt was stretched out of all proportion by her giant baby bump. She looked like she'd swallowed a space hopper. She had a wodge of big rough-edged sheets of paper balanced on top of her bump, and was drawing on them with quill pen and ink. Her multi-coloured hair hung down over her face as she concentrated, and her tattooed arm moved smoothly across the page. The cursed necklace of bad pennies that had been the start (and the end) of last year's adventures dangled out of the top of her T-shirt and glinted its wicked gleam. Emily never had been sure if they'd got them all back after she'd hurled them at the Nocturne and given her a dose of bad luck she'd never forget. They were notoriously hard to count and keep track of.

Emily stayed quiet for a while and watched, surprised by how beautiful her mum's sketches were. Maeve drew fluid lines and shapes that resolved themselves into horses running across the paper. Her sculptures were so wildly out there and bonkers that the perfect horses flowing from her pen were unexpected. Emily's mum didn't look up but still managed to do the annoying mind-reading thing she did (which she vowed wasn't a Pooka power, just 'Ma sense').

'Why so shocked I can draw, darl?'

'Well, it's just . . .'

Emily gestured at the scrap-metal chaos filling the rest of the room.

'Ah, that's later work. This is where I started. Ye've got to know the rules before ye can break them, see.'

Another horse fell from the end of her pen on to the page, and her mum blew on it and passed the rough cartridge paper to Emily to pin up on the wall to dry. There was a chain of horses already there, pinned up side by side. It was like an old animation loop of a horse running across the studio wall. Her mum looked at them and sighed, her hand reaching to rub her swollen belly.

'The only running I'll be doing,' she said, and then her voice hardened. 'And the only running ye'll be doing, unless ye listen to my rules, right?'

'Okay,' said Emily, whose lecture sense was tingling.

'Here's the deal: no nosing, no adventures, and never leave home without yer hedgehog.' She gave Emily her terrifying mum-stare, which could read minds and boil eggs at a hundred yards. 'Are we clear?'

'Crystal.'

'Good. I mean it about the Hog too. Let's face it, he's the only one of ye with any sense.' She intensified the laser squint and Emily was glad that, for once, she hadn't got a guilty conscience. 'Ye go and do yer practice, work on yer hound shape, then back to meet yer da at the curfew time he sets. No side quests. Clear?'

'Cut glass.'

Her mum folded her arms over her bump. Her stare could have penetrated lead plates.

'And absolutely no messing about with the Pooka. Ye steer clear of the clan at all costs, or I'll skin ye.'

Emily twitched. This was a sore spot. The Pooka clan were her mum's family who lived in the Hour, that her mum was in exile from. The only one Emily had met was Uncle Pat, her mum's brother, and a Pooka most disreputable. At the very thought of him, Emily managed a small transformation without magic as her mouth puckered up into a little dog's bottom. Pat had made her feel she'd finally found her family, then he'd locked the door to Midnight in her face. He hadn't been seen since.

'But—'

'I mean it, Em. Not Pat, not none of them, particularly Herself.'

By this, Maeve meant her own mum. It was the only way she'd ever refer to her (apart from 'that stubborn baggage' occasionally). Her mum had fallen out with her and the whole clan big time but Emily had never learnt the full details. Pinning her mum down on family stuff was like juggling a greased weasel.

'But—'

'One more "but" and I'll kick yers.' Her mum was deathly serious. The cursed silver coins around her neck shimmered as she spoke.

Emily's gob was rising. It was a trait she'd inherited from her mum's side of the family; a deep-seated ancestral urge to fire off her mouth like a machine gun at the slightest upset. Her mum had it too, so when they argued it was like playing conkers with hand grenades. Emily was determined not to have an explosion today though – she was so close to getting back into the Midnight Hour.

'*Fine*,' said Emily, in a voice that suggested it was anything but. 'The only reason I'd want to see Pat would be to kick his anyway.'

'Not if I saw him first,' said her mum, fists clenched.

They shared a fierce mutual scowl, but her mum's faded into a more concerned frown.

'Ye don't go looking for him on yer own. Or the rest of them. Ye're not ready yet.' Her mum wasn't using the laser beam now but big sad eyes instead. 'Promise ye won't? It's my condition for letting ye go.'

'I promise I won't go looking for them,' said Emily.

The laser beam returned.

'Oh well, yer good and vague there, aren't ye? Getting the hang of the Pooka-ing already, I see. I think ye need to promise to—'

Just then the baby kicked and Maeve doubled up and knocked the ink pot over and started swearing terribly in Irish, and suddenly everything was chaos and all promises were forgotten.

'Ye think normal babies kick? Try one that's going to grow up to be a horse!' She clutched her side. 'Get me a towel, and yer da. This is all his fault!'

Emily scooted out the room before it became her fault too.

Fizzing with excitement, Emily ran up to her room to tell Hoggins the good news. He was her rescue-and-occasionally-pocket hedgehog, and was currently snoozing on the bed on his hog-blanket, curled up next to Feesh, Emily's cuddly crocodile.

'Hoggins! We get to go! Yes!'

He blinked blearily and closed his eyes again. She could tell he was excited. Emily wasn't entirely convinced that the Hog wasn't a little bit magic. There'd been a few odd moments on her last adventure but nothing to put her finger on. Her mum swore he was 'just a normal hedgepig' but she could not, of course, be trusted in the slightest. If the Hog knew anything more, he certainly wasn't saying.

A whirlwind of packing took place as she stuffed her bag with the essentials of Midnight Hour existence (book to read, snacks, garlic, auxiliary snacks, crucifix, back-up auxiliary snacks, crisp sandwich, Library card, entire packet of biscuits). She tugged on her clompiest boots (because, of course, big boots were best), the bomber jacket she'd swiped from her mum, and grabbed the flat cap her dad hadn't noticed was missing yet. She made a point of leaving her mobile phone on her bedside table though. Magic and technology were a literally explosive combination.

All set, she threw herself on the bed to snoogle Feesh, and the Hog yipped and grizzled as the impact bounced him in the air. 'Sorry Hoggins, come here.' She held out a hand and, after giving her some side-eye, he shuffled his small, warm weight into it.

'Adventure buddies,' she whispered as she stroked his little nose. She was going back to the Midnight Hour. She was going to be magic again.

CHAPTER 2

It was one minute to midnight and Emily was standing with her dad in a dark alley at the only remaining back door of a post office which didn't exist anymore. She held a skull-fobbed key close to the lock and waited for the right moment. Getting into the Midnight Hour wasn't easy. The right door had to be unlocked with the right key exactly at midnight as Big Ben chimed.

As she waited in the shadow of the dome of St Paul's, she thought of the first time she'd opened this door, and how different it had been. She shuddered at the memory of the roar and the sheer animal stink of the Bear – the terri-fying were-beast who'd been chasing her. The haunting sound of the quarter chimes echoing in the air brought her back to the present and she slid the key in. As the bongs reverberated into the night, marking midnight for all of London, she turned the key fully and the door opened. A gust of sorcery washed over her, making her skin tingle. The Pooka part of her was coming alive once more. Grinning, she stepped through into the heart of the Night Post, into the Midnight Hour.

Once inside, Emily's dad shrugged off his coat to reveal his black Night Post uniform with the silver skull buttons. He popped his peaked cap on and tipped her a wink as they entered the buzzing mayhem of the sorting room. Emily smiled as the madness of it boiled around them. This was the first place she had seen real magic, and it would always be special to her. It was full of a whirl of people and post, letters and lycanthropes, all alight with urgency to get ready for the next round of deliveries. Bats swooped flying letters from the air and into postbags, and the old pneumatic tubes clanked and spat floods of post on to the already crowded sorting desks, most of it spilling straight on to the floor. Everywhere was the hiss and fizz of magic, major and minor, as the packages wriggled, popped, fizzed and, in some cases, tried to leg it.

The staff smiled and waved at her. Jonesy, the post troll, even picked her up for a squeeze, but it was nothing compared to how her dad was treated. As they headed across the floor to his section, there were a host of hellos, tipped caps, curtseys, and firm nods of mutual respect. Outside the Midnight Hour her dad was a quiet man who spent a lot of time in his potting shed thinking about compost, but inside he was the Dangerous Deliveries Specialist and had rock-star status. Emily thought this might be even weirder than magic being real.

Her apparently cool dad leant his bike against the wall, and put a hand on her shoulder.

'Right, tell me how your curfew works.'

'Oh, come on. We've been over this.'

'Tell me.' He was quiet but insistent.

'Fine. I have the night watch.' She rummaged in her pocket and pulled it out by its chain. The night watches were the magic timepieces used to tell the time in both worlds. She opened the silver case and a miniature Big Ben spiralled up from it with a distant chiming noise. She squinted at the four dials.

Time flowed differently in the Hour, in fact it hardly flowed at all, so the time outside flowed on like a stream, or toffee, or whatever. She'd never got the hang of the magic science behind it, but she knew it moved quicker outside than in here, so you had to be careful not to be gone too long.

'And?

'And I go and practise but keep an eye on the watch, and

when the alarm you've set at a time *way* too early goes off, I will be sat here, waiting for you, so we can go home together.' She gave him her widest, brightest smile. 'Because I am extremely trustworthy and reliable.'

He gave her a knowing look, then nodded.

'Good. Don't mess this up, Puzzle. I promised your mum you wouldn't, and I don't want to have to go and live in the shed.'

'You'd love living in the shed. Think of the extra composting time.'

'Hmmm.'

He leant down and gave her a big hug, and then casually strolled off with his bike towards an evening of terrible danger.

'Yoo hoo, Emily!'

A voice split the air and Emily jumped. It was the echoingly loud voice of the very posh; people for whom normal volume rules did not apply. It was her friend, Japonica, who was second in command at the post office, under the ghastly Postmaster.

'Japonica!' They ran towards each other and hugged. She smiled up at Japonica, who was considerably taller than her. Japonica's skin was black as night, her eyes red as burning embers, and her teeth were sharp and white as a shark's. She always looked like that though, so what was different?

'Wait . . .' Emily stepped back to look her up and down. Japonica normally wore a practical but still-constricting dress of blackened lace, but instead . . . 'Are those trousers?'

Japonica flushed and gave a small twirl. They were made of a thick dark blue material almost hidden beneath a swathe of tweed pockets. They were totally shapeless, and probably sturdy enough to fend off bullets, let alone the weather, but they were definitely trousers.

'Yes. I was rather taken with yours, you know. So practical.' Japonica's eyes blazed with enthusiasm. 'I was all set to have some run up, then a chap on the Night Market proved to be selling these in just the right size.' She jammed her thumbs in the top pockets and twirled again, grinning.

'I had to adjust the pockets, of course. One can never have enough pockets.'

Emily thought maybe you could, but didn't like to say.

'They're fabulous!'

Japonica coughed with embarrassment, and flapped her hand to make Emily stop.

'Quite a few of the other gals have taken to them too. They're a wonder. Ladders are no longer a potential moral disaster, and riding a bicycle has become a greatly simpler exercise.'

'But what about the Postmaster?' The ghastly shouting corpse who was in charge of the Night Post would surely not have taken kindly to this type of innovation.

'Oh, he went to pieces about the whole thing. Took ages to find all the bits too, I must say.'

Japonica plucked a piece of fluff from her jacket, and studied it.

'Actually, I've been terribly busy so I haven't quite got round to putting him together again yet. He's in a big jar by the door.'

She pointed. A very large, very solid jar stood there. It had a thick cork jammed in the neck, and a number of large parcels stacked on top, holding it closed. The whole pile was vibrating and there was a distant blocked plumbing kind of noise coming from the jar.

'I'm running the place in the meanwhile. Things are ever so much more efficient round here now.'

Their eyes met and Japonica grinned. Her smile was as unexpectedly pointy and sharp as when Emily had first seen it, but she couldn't imagine how she'd ever found it scary now. Japonica squeezed her hand.

'Do come back for tea later. I've got those tiny cakes you like.'

Emily always shivered when she stepped back out into the moonlight of the Midnight Hour, no matter how many times she did it. The moon here was larger than she'd ever seen it at home, and shone down with a stark intensity nearly as bright as daylight. It left sharp, solid shadows where it fell, turning all to bone and blackness as it silvered the world.

It was always full moon, and always, always midnight in this London. The spell cast by Big Ben (or the Great Working, as it was known here) had frozen a moment of time for ever. This was the city of the Night Folk though, and so the streets were still crowded. All the world comes to London, her dad used to say. Here, beneath the moon in this gaslit London, all the *under*world had come instead. The Night Folk thronged around and their languages washed over her, cracked out in rock-speak by trolls, liquid splashing trills from nereids, and fluting whistles from green children of the woods.

Emily was about to barge her way into the crowd when she remembered she was hatless. Everyone in the Hour wore a hat – it was a Victorian thing – so wearing one doubled as a cunning disguise against those who weren't keen on humans (or daysies, as they called them), or were possibly too keen in a 'like to have you for dinner and not in a good way' sense. She grabbed her flat cap out of her pocket and jammed it on her head. She then made her elbows pointy and squirmed and dodged her way through the busy streets, weaving through goblins and boggarts, ducking damply past bickering greenteeth and kappa, and slaloming through a staggering copse of dryads out on a hedge-do. The Pooka part of her was expanding now, tasting and breathing magic once again, and it loved to move. It found gaps and squiggled through them better than she ever could and so she flowed through the hustle and bustle like a chunky otter in a stream.

By the time she cleared the busy bit of town and got out to Gloomsbury, she was sweating but grinning with the pleasure of it. Only as she arrived at the private walled garden of Mecklenburgh Square where her mum had told her to practise did her smile slip. She used her mum's skeleton key (made from real skeletons) to open the metal gate and slip through into the quiet oasis of trees and lawns and paths. She looked around at the green space she was supposed to do her hound homework in and, with a whimper, her Pooka-self curled into a ball and tucked itself way back down inside her. Not a great start.

All Pooka had three shapes – hare, hound and horse. She'd done the hare, just about, and her mum wanted her to move on to the hound shape. When her mum demonstrated it she'd switched forms with a flicker you'd have missed if you blinked. From mum to dog, boom. Maeve became a sleek, jet-black longdog, a massive demonic greyhound, like a shadow walking. She was soundless and swift and she ran so fast her red eyes seemed to bleed out in a crimson line behind her. She was beautiful.

Sleek, soundless and beautiful were not words that

would describe Emily's attempts to transform into a hound. Her efforts were, according to her mum, 'a work in progress'. What this appeared to mean was that Emily couldn't do it at all. She wasn't any good at dogs. Which was a shame, as she really liked them. Apparently turning into one was much harder than wanting to be more receptive to tummy rubs though. It just left her with a stinking headache and an urge to wee up lamp posts.

Now, stood here alone without her mum's infuriating but insistent encouragement, she was all of a sudden seized with the urge to give up. If she couldn't do it, what was the point? She was about to find a tree to sit under and get involved in some serious self-pity when she was disturbed by a burst of motion and furious squeaking from inside her jacket pocket. She slipped her hand in and found the Hog, wedged upside down and pedalling furiously.

'Oh Hoggins, what *are* you doing? Are you stuck?'

She extricated him gently then popped him, right side up, on her palm. His small warm weight shifted from paw to paw and front to back as he shivered and shuffled all his spines back to where they should be. He glared at her, making it clear this had never happened. She pressed her lips together so she wouldn't smile, and stroked his little nose with a fingertip. He rumbled like a tiny thundercloud as she held him up to eye level.

'Hoggins, I'm struggling here. The whole changing into

other things thing is kind of a . . . thing. When I wasn't allowed in the Hour anymore, it seemed very important I should be, but now . . .'

She frowned and chewed her lip. He gazed up at her, not unkindly.

'I mean, even the hare is a problem. I managed when I was terrified, but now . . . like, one in five is good? And that's only if Mum jumps out and shouts "boo". She gave a deep sigh. 'I could try the hound I guess, but it's all really quite difficult and . . .'

The Hog squinted at her a bit.

'I know, I know, it's all practice and everything, but it gives me a thumping headache and I . . .'

The expression on the small brown face was now very squinty indeed.

'Yeah, you're right, you're right. I should at least give it a go while we're here.'

He scrunched his nose at her one more time.

'Thanks Hoggins, good chat.'

She laid her jacket on the floor and set him down on it carefully, a spiky brown island in a sea of orange lining. She had promised she wouldn't transform with him after last time, when he was *very* put out by going wherever it was her clothes went when she changed. The 'mystic laundry cupboard', her mum called it. (Her mum had a theory they came back cleaner than before and it might be easier than washing, but she was a mad Irish woman of supernatural origin and not to be trusted.) Emily went and stood at the edge of the lawns that filled the centre of the gardens. In the middle under tall trees was a statue of a lady in a flowing dress, holding a sword above her head with both hands. She sighed, nodded to the statue lady, then clenched her fists.

'Right, okay, you can do this. Think doggy thoughts. Get your woof on.'

She closed her eyes and reached down inside herself to where her other shapes lived. Finding the hare was easy enough, whiskers and ears a-twitch and mercurially alive and ready to bound; the horse was far beyond her reach in the darkness, a glimpse of thick mane and muscled legs full of speed and power; last of the triple forms and tantalisingly close now was the hound. It sat inside her, curled up, all sharp teeth and lolling tongue, fleet flanks and whipping tail. She grasped it, more firmly than she'd ever managed to before, and strained to pull it over her head as if it were a huge jumper. An electric thrill shot through her as it started to open, and her senses prickled as they came alive, and the night smelt different and she was so nearly there, she was going to do it, not like all those other failures. Then, at the thought of failure, she hesitated and the sleek fur pulled back through her fingers, and the jumper was tugged up and away from her, and the shape left her, and she tumbled back into her own body. All of a sudden the night smelt the same as it always had, her head was pulsing with a thick electric zap, her teeth were aching and she'd failed again.

'Urgh!' she barked, which was as close as she was going to get to dog noise. She collapsed to her knees and pounded her fists on the soggy turf. Why couldn't she get it? She held it inside her, or outside her, or wherever it actually was, but couldn't find her way into it. Was it because she was only half Pooka? Maybe she just didn't have enough magic to make it work?

She flopped back in the grass, not caring about getting soggy, and lay still and waited for her head to stop throbbing. She could hear the gentle snuffling of Hoggins behind her and the cool damp grass was soothing her head, when a sudden grating, grinding noise came from close by. She sat up with a jerk, but there were just trees and grass and the statue lady . . . hang on. The sword was no longer pointing at the sky. It was pointing straight at her, and the serene face behind it had twisted into what might have been a scream or shout, with a gaping open mouth. Emily's headache was replaced by a chill coursing straight down her back.

The noise came again. Heavy stone moving on heavy stone and this time she saw it. The statue was moving. It glared straight at her with blind eyes, took one marbled hand off the sword hilt and groped towards her. All the time its mouth opened and closed, wailing a silent scream. Emily let go a little scream herself that definitely wasn't silent.

'Oh, that is never right.'

CHAPTER 3

E mily had seen far too much *Doctor Who* to even
think about blinking. She inched back towards the
Hog, moving on her hands, wonky crab style. The
statue was frantic now, the sword swinging as its other
hand clawed for her. Emily touched her jacket and she
flipped over instantly, bundled it around the Hog who
squeaked with surprise, grabbed her bag and ran as fast as
she could for the park gate. Behind her the sound of
tortured stone, and a resounding thud which might have
been a very heavy statue leaping from its podium. The skin
on the back of her neck crawled as she waited to feel stone
fingers grab her any second. She thudded into the gate, and

risked a glance back as she scrabbled to open it.

The statue was not right behind her but had fallen on the floor by its pedestal. The mouth was far too wide open in a silent scream and its hand was still reaching for her. She hurled herself through the gate and slammed it behind her. Now, she decided, might be a nice time to go for a run, for no reason other than health purposes, obviously.

She was several streets away when she risked stopping to get her breath back, and to de-bundle a very put-out Hoggins. That had been freaky, even for the Midnight Hour. The stone of the statue had flowed as it moved, and its screaming face . . . *ugh*. Training was blown for the evening and a tiny part of her whispered that she was glad to have a good excuse to not try changing again. She pretended not to hear it. What she could hear however was her tummy rumbling. Fear, as ever, had made her hungry. Japonica's earlier offer of tea and tiny cakes sounded pretty great right now. In the meanwhile, it was emergency biscuit time.

She was rooting in her bag when it started to vibrate. She rummaged and pulled out her Library card, the thick cardboard token the Library herself had given to her after she'd helped save the world. (The Library was also a person. It was complicated.) It showed Emily was a Librarian, and gave her kind-of secret agent status. It was one of life's deep unfairnesses that she couldn't tell anyone at school about this. The card was buzzing in her hand and scratchy black handwriting appeared on it, scrawled by an invisible pen:

Meet me at Paternoster Row immediately

She'd know the antiquated writing anywhere. It was the Library herself.

'Well, that's new. What does Bookerella want?'

Emily pulled her night watch out and peered at it.

'Hoggins, we've still got ages. I guess I can go and see what she wants.' She frowned. 'There is literally zero chance of her having cake though.'

She'd asked directions from a passing boojum, and getting to Paternoster Row meant going back most of the way towards the Night Post. As she neared it, she followed her nose towards the dome of St Paul's, slipping through the smoke and fog of the side alleys surrounding it. The mighty roar of London ran round, the sound of an unseen ocean, but the long archway passage she walked into was quiet enough to hear the echo of her own footfalls. There was another noise too, not the tides of London behind her, but a dry rustling noise ahead. It grew louder, a gentle flutter filling her ears, like somebody riffling paper. Lots of paper. She emerged from the arch on to Paternoster Row and stopped in her tracks.

'Whoa,' said Emily.

The papery rustle filled the air, and it was the sound of books; not books being made or being flicked through, but books *moving*. There were even more books here than in the library that the Library lived in. (Or that the Library *was*; she'd never quite wrapped her head around it.) A waterfall of books, a positive deluge of them, and oh, what books.

The long, dark street ahead of her was lined with bookshops, and in every shop window there were books flapping and writhing, pressing against the glass like puppies at the pet shop waiting to be taken home. Outside each shop were street tables filled with piles of books; books in cages like square leather hamsters, angry snapping guard dog books on chains, and – she ducked, as a shape veered close to her head – books flying like birds. The gloomy air of the street was full of flying books, a whole flock of them, fluttering from stand to stand, settling on the occasional shoulder, or sometimes dive-bombing from a great height, causing people to duck and curse. Each of the book merchants had a harassed-looking apprentice outside holding long wooden poles with brass-hooped nets, or complicated grabbing mechanisms. The net-boys jogged up and down the street, attempting to herd the books that had gone too far, or collar the ones their customers were pointing at. The night air was full of paper birds with leather wings, but without a single tweet or chirp; the only sounds the constant dry flapping of pages and the curses of the net-boys.

She wandered down Paternoster Row, gaping in wonder. The street was narrow, lined with tall buildings that left it gloomy and shadowed, and lit only by the warm light flooding from the glass shopfronts. Each book merchant's window had a boldly lettered sign above it – Skullastic, Grotledge, Hatchet, Foulshed & Spawn – and their window displays promised marvels. Brightly coloured books of sorcery thrummed their marbled covers like exotic butterflies, while darker necromantic tomes hung upside down under the shelves and brooded in the shadows. On the tables, scrolls unrolled and books flicked open as she walked along, illuminated letters fountaining up and out of them, falling back into the pages as she passed.

Over the street ahead of her, the books were acting differently. Rather than flapping around on their own, they were flocking together in bigger groups in the air, then diving, lifting and turning, their dark covers and white pages creating flickering shapes and patterns, like murmurating starlings coming in to roost. They rolled and swooped and darkened the air, all mobbing over one spot. The Library had arrived.

She was further up the street, a shock of long black hair

swaying head and shoulders above anyone else in the small crowd of book browsers. She was drifting along, clad in the usual white tattered lace of what might have once been a wedding dress, trailing her finger across the covers of books. The stallholders were obviously used to this and simply tipped their caps or bonnets as she passed by. The books gathered above her in their twisting flock, never touching but flying close for her attention. At one point, they all swooped down and pulsed out on either side of the Library, and for a moment she had huge paper wings. The Library wasn't much for smiling, but her face was more content than usual when Emily walked over to her.

'Word, booky,' said Emily. 'Get it? No?'

In classic Library style, instead of replying, she turned and entered the nearest bookshop, 'D. Read & Co', according to the sign. She had to duck to get under the door frame. Emily sighed and followed her in.

Inside, the shop had high ceilings and the walls were lined all the way to the roof with shelves stuffed with shifting, rustling books. The flustered proprietor, a large red manticore with a fancy hat, bowed so deeply his hat fell off, but the Library breezed past him without a word. He was soon distracted by a rush of flying books from other shops trying to follow the Library into his, and a scrum of net-boys forming in his doorway. Emily gave him a *whaddyagonna do?* shrug, and followed the Library down the winding passages lined with whispering books until she finally halted in a dark, scroll-lined alcove.

'Woe, destruction, ruin and decay: The worst is death, and death will have his day,' the Library said with quiet urgency.

'Oh, I'm fine thank you, how are you?' said Emily.

'Doomsday is near. Die all, die merrily.' The Library's usually impassive face was clouded with shadows.

'Come on, we talked about the quoting thing, didn't we?' Emily gave a long-suffering sigh. 'Less doom, more details please.'

'There is a threat hanging over this whole world.' The Library's long-fingered hand touched Emily's arm as she spoke.

'Ah man, that's not a quote is it?' said Emily. 'I thought things were okay now? What with all the dropping a bell on your evil sister and stuff.'

The Library's face crumpled. Emily kicked herself. *Too soon.* Must remember not to rub in the bell thing. She was still recovering from it all herself – the terrible stand-off she'd had against the Nocturne at the top of Big Ben was now level pegging with 'chased by a bear' as her worst stress dream ever. They had taken over from her 'naked at school' one and everything.

'I'm sorry, that was like, totally insensitive. I just mean, I thought you, we, were all safe again now?'

'We are, most likely, safe from my sister for now. She was made incorporeal by your attack, and it takes even our kind a long time to recover from that.' There were fewer flying books in here; most of them roosted contentedly on their home shelves, but smaller tomes fluttered around the Library as she spoke, like paper moths drawn to a lantern. Her thin lips pursed. 'She struck down our sister in the War for the Hour, and Art has still not re-formed.'

The War had been between the Older Powers: the Sisters Three, Music, Art and Language. Language, or the Library as Emily knew her, and her sister Art created the Midnight Hour spell to offer refuge to the Night Folk from a world where magic was disappearing. But Music, or the Nocturne as she was known now, had refused to give up her freedom. The war had been won, and the Midnight Hour created, but there had been terrible losses on both sides, including Art.

There was a long pause in which the Library reached up and gently stroked a tiny booklet that had landed on her shoulder. Emily had a sudden realization that the Library was all alone. The only one of her kind left, with the rest of her family blown to bits or enemies or both, with no one who could understand what it was to be her. She was trying to think of what to say when the Library continued.

'But there are others who share the Nocturne's goal, who feel trapped in this Midnight world and would do much to leave it. They could doom us all.'

'How d'you mean?' said Emily.

The Library beckoned her closer.

'Strange and arcane artefacts have been found in this world. They throb with the contained energy of the Daylight realm and mean that someone has reached beyond the Great Working to pull them into this world for some dread purpose.'

'Blimey,' said Emily.

'Gaze upon them in fear.'

The Library's hands blurred for a second and then they were full of the arcane artefacts. She held them out to Emily, who flinched.

'Your thoughts?' said the Library. She looked deathly serious, which was pretty serious indeed for someone who never really looked anything else but.

'Erm, well, that's a really old digital watch, that's a yoyo and that . . .' Emily leant in. 'Hmmm . . . let me see, I'll need to examine these more closely.'

She picked up the dun-coloured foil wrapper and eased the edges apart with an audible hiss of air. She bent her head over it and sniffed. The Library leant in too, fascinated.

'I think it's . . . One final test to be sure . . .'

She teased out one of the identical dry circular formations from inside the foil, popped it in her mouth and crunched away.

'Mmmm, yup, definitely beef Hula Hoops. Want one?'

The Library stared down her long nose and didn't answer.

'Nope? Suit yourself. I'll keep them for further study. Let you know what I find.' She crunched as quietly as she could. 'Everything here is just tat from my world. They're not magic or anything. So, no doomy doom, right?'

The Library's face was thunderous, and her eyes flickered with the black ink Emily never liked to see. The Library was made up of all the words in the world, and she was sometimes overwhelmed by them.

'Wrong. This is exactly as I feared. They are from outside.'

'Yeah, but so am I. What's the problem?' She examined the digital watch more closely, and frowned around a mouthful of Hula Hoops. 'Hey, this is working. I thought technology blew up here?'

'You are correct, it should not survive the ambient level of magic.'

Emily remembered her old mobile phone blackening and burning in her hand and winced.

'Sooo . . . ?' said Emily.

'It means the magic this place, this great spell, was built to preserve is leaking out,' the Library whispered. 'I have warded all the exit doors after the Nocturne's crimes, but these artefacts prove there is another way in, a tear in time.'

'Ah. That's bad, right?'

'It is disastrous. The more the tear is used, the worse the magic leak gets. Without magic, there is no Midnight Hour, so we *must* stop it.'

The Library unfolded to her full height, as if they were about to set out to stop it immediately. The booklet flapped off from her shoulder, disturbed. Emily took a step back, folded her arms, and glared up (a long way up) at her.

'What do you mean, *we*, bookface?'

'You are clearly the person who must look into this.' The Library spoke like she was explaining to a child (which she technically was).

Emily let out the hiss of a cat spotting its arch-enemy cat from over the road.

'Pump your brakes, booky! Don't Dumbledore me! There must be a load of people you can ask who aren't still at school. Why me?'

'Only you can recognize these things with any certainty.' The Library quirked her lips in what was almost a smile. 'And you seem to have a knack for effortlessly finding trouble. I suspect it's a family trait.'

'Absolutely not! I've done all the hero thing already and I nearly got eaten, like, three times. That shouldn't happen even once!' Emily's gob was about to make its presence known. Thinking about getting eaten did it every time.

The Library said nothing, merely stared at her, and a

hot flush prickled across Emily's cheeks.

'What are you doing?'

'I am giving you a hard stare,' the Library said, still inflicting the beady eye on her, 'as recommended by the excellent bear, Paddington, from your last batch of books.'

'Well, stop it.' Emily waved a hand between them as if to clear flies. 'I still don't see why it has to be me.'

The Library's hand flickered, there was a tug at Emily's pocket and her Library card was dancing between the Library's fingers like a magician's coin.

'Oi, that's mine—' Emily stopped as the Library arched one of her perfect eyebrows at her.

'What did you think? That it was a souvenir? I awarded you a card firstly because you did this realm a great service, but also because you could do us *further* service.' She held the card still and they both stared at it. 'It confers great privilege, yes, but with great privilege . . .'

'Comes great responsibility,' said Emily.

The Library nodded in appreciation. She liked a good quote. 'Well put,' she said.

'Swiped it from a comic,' said Emily. 'Look, I want to help, I do, but I'm famously not that responsible. I've got school reports proving it and everything.'

'I wish only for you to identify these objects in the Midnight world and trace their source. Once you find the location of this tear in time, then, well . . .'

The Library's face creased in worry. She was getting a full emotional workout today.

'It was my sister Art, not I, who was the architect of the Great Working, but I will try to re-knit it nonetheless. This is why you must not delay!'

'Fine. *Fine.* I'm totally on an adventure-banning curfew though, so I can only help for a bit tonight. Best if we never mention this to my dad either, cool?' She frowned. 'Or he'll do that dreadful "extra-quiet but deeply disappointed" thing he does.'

'I thank you. Good hunting,' said the Library.

There was a sudden kerfuffle from Emily's left as a flapping book collided with a table and the piles teetered dangerously close to falling. She turned to look, and when she turned back the Library was gone.

'Whoa, total Batman move,' she said, then held her hands out in exasperation to someone who was no longer there.

'Hang on, where am I supposed to start?' But it was too late.

'Great. Just great. Textbook enigmatic. Blooming immortal timeless demigod-like presences . . .'

She was still muttering as she left the shop, then brightened up as she remembered the rest of the Hula Hoops. She slipped one into her pocket for the Hog, put one on the end of each of her fingers, and left Paternoster Row behind, munching, deep in thought.

'If we're detectives now, Hog, and we *definitely* are, then what we need is a glamorous assistant.'

She took the enthusiastic crunches coming from her pocket as agreement.

'I know just the person!'

CHAPTER 4

The door of the office of Probationary Inspector Tarkus Poswa crashed open. It caused the inspector to let out a high-pitched shriek, bang his knees on the desk and spill his tea on his paperwork and into his lap. The open doorway was filled by a short sturdy figure with outstretched arms, and a too-loud voice.

'Great news!' Emily shouted.

Tarkus was half out of his chair, frantically mopping tea off his files while jiggling to keep the tea-heated parts of his trousers off anything sensitive. Emily shrugged and carried on.

'I'm getting the team back together for one last heist,

and you're in.'

She waited for a response. He picked up his soggy and dripping paperwork, sighed and dropped it into the bin. His brown skin glowed from the flicker of flame in his yellow eyes. The room filled with the bitter smell of scorched lemon rind. Tarkus was a ghûl, a type of Night Folk who ate flowers and had a magical command of scents. He was the only person Emily knew who could actually smell angry.

'I'm not entirely sure what that means but, on principle, absolutely not.'

'But the team! A new investigation!'

She plonked herself on the corner of his desk and gave him the big puppy eyes. He sat back down in his chair, wincing at his hot wet trousers, and gave her a look which could have been described as suspicious. She was getting a lot of those today.

'What team? The hapless, long-suffering policeman and the bad-luck vortex?'

'I am not a vortex!' She swung her feet where they hung off the desk. 'What's a vortex?'

He ignored her, leant back into his chair and steepled his fingers under his nose, resting them on his ill-advised scraggy moustache. It looked a lot like his lecture pose.

'It is a miracle I survived our last shenanigan. Assaulted multiple times, plunged into sewage, a terrifying unsafe flight on an ill-piloted bicycle, and hand-to-hand combat with a bear.'

He shook his head slowly. It *was* his lecture pose.

'I still have nightmares about falling down that drop, and everything hurts in my arm and side when it's cold, and IT'S ALWAYS COLD HERE BECAUSE IT'S STUPID LONDON.'

He blanched, shocked at the level of his own voice. There was an afterwash of the astringent scent of nettles. Emily, whose eyes were still wide from the unexpected explosion, leant forward, elbows on her knees.

'Tough day at the office?' she said.

He sighed. 'Yes. Apologies. I am exhausted from doing extra shifts on the new door watch and it makes me very grumpy.'

'Grumpy's totally my job.'

He raised his head and smiled, a ray of sunshine on a winter's day.

'Indeed. Would you like tea? My trousers appear to have drunk my last cup.'

'Yes, please. And cake, obvs.'

She bounced off the desk and grabbed a spare chair. He opened a drawer and produced another cup and a large square tin. He filled both cups from the teapot on the side, and slid one and the tin over to Emily, who was staring into a silver compact case she'd picked up off his desk.

'Ooooh, swirly!'

'Do you mind not playing with the hypno-mirror, please?' He reached over and yoinked it out of her paws. 'It's not a toy, it's restricted police mind-control equipment.'

'But I'm Pooka-immune, it just makes me giddy,' she said giddily.

'Immune, or merely a lack of mind to control? We shall never know.'

Emily nodded in appreciation. Snappy comeback.

'Got any milk?' she said.

'It's a disgusting abomination to put the squeezings of a cow into good tea.'

'I'll take that as a no.' She sniffed her cup, wrinkled her nose, then slurped. Her whole face crinkled up. 'What is this? It's not Tetley.'

'It's dandelion. There's seed cake too.'

Emily opened the tin and eyed the contents suspiciously.

'There's a lot more seeds than cake, is all I'm saying. What's wrong with Hobnobs?'

'If you don't want it . . .'

He reached for the tin.

'I never said that,' said Emily as she pulled it out of his reach and grabbed a slice.

'Try dipping it in the tea. It's how we have it at home.'

She squinted at him in case he was engaged in what her mum would call 'funny business', then gingerly dipped the corner of the seedy cake into the golden brew. She tasted it, chewed slowly and then her face lit up as her mouth filled with honeyed gold.

'Hey, that's actually pretty good.'

Tarkus pinched a thumb and forefinger together and inclined his head. 'Both my mother and my ancestral line thank you for your seal of approval.'

They both dipped and slurped. Emily snapped a corner off her cake, dipped it, then held it by her Hog pocket. It was pulled from her fingers by small but powerful jaws.

'So what's all this door watch lark then?' Emily said, around a mouthful of soggy cake.

'Ever since the Nocturne sneaked music in from outside and nearly collapsed the Great Working, the Library has altered the spell to ward all the doors. No one can get out now without the counter-charm.' He gestured at himself, in faux-grandeur. 'Of course, someone has to check all those doors are actually locked. So, you are talking to the new Probationary Inspector in charge of Doors, Portals, Gates, and other Means of Egress.'

She narrowed her eyes. 'What have birds got to do with it?'

'What on Luna are you talking about?' he said.

'Egret's a bird, isn't it?'

'Egress. *Egress!*' A vein pulsed in his forehead. 'To leave, or exit. Something one goes out of! *Egress.*'

'Oh, right, gotcha. Birds would have been more fun though, right?'

'You're undoubtedly correct.' He rubbed his head wearily. 'Do you know how many doors in our London are still active in yours?'

You could only get into Midnight London through old doors that still existed in both times, 1859 and the present, but London was an old city . . .

'Ermmm . . . quite a lot?'

'Really substantially more than quite a lot, in fact. I'd go as far as to say there are in fact, exactly –' he paused, holding a finger aloft in thought – 'very, very, many, many lots, and I must make sure they are all locked and warded.'

He reached down into his desk drawer and produced a key chain, festooned with very very many many lots of tiny keys of all shapes and sizes, and with a single large and glowing one that literally outshone them all. It was pearlescent and throbbed with the same emerald-green sorcerous light which wreathed Big Ben in this world.

'Cor, what's that one open?'

He hefted it in his hand and pursed his lips.

'*Anything.* It's the Master Key, part of the original spell of the Great Working. It has power over any door, portal or *egress.*' He enunciated the last word carefully. 'More importantly, it can lock anything too.'

'Ooh, one key to rule them all!'

'Eh?'

'Never mind.'

'The job and the rank is a great honour. No one of my background has ever been advanced this quickly before.' He was hollow-eyed. 'It is also awful. *Awful.* The doors are everywhere. They're endless . . .'

He gripped his cup with both hands and slurped at it.

'Wow.' She paused, thinking about how best to be supportive at what was obviously a difficult time. 'So the inspector's job really opened some doors for you then?'

He didn't look up, but his pointy ears stiffened and the flare of his eyes lighting up to full burn glinted off the white china of the cup.

'I am legally allowed to lock you up for ever and no one could do anything. They would never find you.'

She grinned.

'Are you saying you'd lock the door and throw away the key?'

He groaned and rested his head on the desk blotter. A little more tea slopped out but he didn't seem to notice or care.

'What was it I did earlier on the karmic wheel for you to be a presence in my life? Did I perhaps commit some unholy genocide? Crush one of the holy flowers beneath an uncaring heel? What was it?'

'What if I had a job that meant you could come and help me and not have to do anything involving doors?'

His head twitched on the desk, then rolled to one side revealing just one flickering flame of an eye.

'No doors?'

'No doors.'

He sat up and glared at her.

'Tell me more of this dreadful proposition that will doubtless imperil my existence.'

'It's a mission of utmost importance from the Library!'

Tarkus let out a deep, sighing breath and rubbed at his barely recovered ribs.

'Go on.'

Soon, they were walking out of the Night Watch station into the cool air of the street. Tarkus winced as the chilly breeze hit his still-damp trousers. He pulled his thick police cape tighter around him and huddled under his large blue helmet.

'So, where are we supposed to start?' he said. 'I could quiz the local Watchmen and see if they've spotted anything unusual?'

'Don't worry, Watson. Sherlock has a plan.'

He shook his head. 'English may be a language lacking in all romance, but I wish you would use it occasionally. What?'

'I, a genius –' she tapped herself on the chest – 'have spotted a clue that you, a doofus –' she gestured grandly at him – 'have failed to.'

He gestured back, rudely, but she magnanimously ignored it. 'Again, *what*?'

'When I met Japonica earlier, her new trousers, under all those pockets, were *new*. They're what we call "jeans". I've only just twigged after the Library talking about Daylight stuff being brought in.' She grinned. 'Now, Japonica said they were from the Night Market. Do you know where that is?'

'I do, yes, but –' his mouth gaped at the injustice – 'I wasn't even with you then and you hadn't told me that you'd seen—'

'Enough excuses, Watson. You must try harder next time. As senior officer here, I shall be taking notes.'

'Oh, you are not in charge! I'm the trained officer, you're a horrific liability!'

'That will be one of my first notes,' she said as she strode off down the street.

Tarkus rested his forehead on his clenched fist for a moment, then walked after her, shouting.

'It's not that way! Come back!'

CHAPTER 5

'So it's called the Night Market, but it's *always* night here, right?'

'Yes,' said Tarkus.

After some redirection, they were now headed straight towards the Night Market, which was apparently in the charmingly named Spittle Fields.

'So calling everything "night" seems a bit . . . extra. We –' she waved a hand at herself to indicate general humanity without fangs – 'don't call all our stuff the "day police" or the "day Tesco" or whatever.'

'Well . . .' Tarkus paused. 'Many of these institutions were established before the Midnight Hour came to be, you understand. The Night Post has long served the community and the Night Market is—'

'Good for night shopping for Night Folk,' Emily said pointedly. 'Perhaps to buy night things for night time?'

'All right, all right,' said Tarkus testily. 'I'll grant it's quite . . . uniformly nighty, but you're dealing with semi-immortal denizens of the ni— dark. Imagination isn't one of their strong points.'

'Mmmhmm,' said Emily, in a small noise that contained a world of smug victory. 'Fair enough. Well, I'm starving, so hopefully we'll be able to get some night nosh from the night chippy and wash it down with some night pop.'

'I warn you, my patience is not unlimited,' said Tarkus. 'I can make you smell like dog poo for days if you push me too far.'

'Night Watchman threatens night niff,' said Emily, then shrieked and sprinted ahead, as Tarkus grabbed for her, his eyes glowing.

'Night attack!' she yelled as she legged it, cackling. She put the brakes on as she rounded a corner and saw the Night Market stretching ahead of her.

It sat in a wide open space at the junction of a number of streets, and pulsed with life (and undeath) and noise. It seethed and heaved, an upended ants' nest with Night Folk scurrying everywhere in between a multitude of tents, stalls, huts, barrows, counters, wagons, concessions, tables, and people just straight-up holding weird stuff out and yelling it was for sale. It was Halloween ball meets travelling fair, with the Black Friday sales sprinkled on top. Emily gazed at it all, stumped.

'Well, all my Christmas shopping worries have been solved for ever, but this is going to be harder than I thought. It's huge.'

Even standing still on the outskirts was difficult. They were getting buffeted by crowds of people headed in or out of the market, and had to start moving again.

'What are we looking for anyway? More of those blue breeches?' said Tarkus.

'*Jeans.* Maybe, but other stuff too. Modern stuff – I mean, weird stuff to you.'

She rummaged through her bag as they walked and held things up to demonstrate.

'Bright colours, plastic – I mean this kind of glossy shiny stuff – and anything with a screen or that bleeps.'

He gingerly poked her cow-shaped plastic lunchbox with his finger. She held up the empty crisp packet from earlier.

'It is particularly important you look for these, but full ones. Very important evidence.'

'Right, got it. Weird outside stuff that smells funny.'

'Does it?'

'Yes, they smell . . .' He clicked his fingers as he groped

for the words. 'Your language is inadequate, but they smell sideways and hot and wrong. You people don't use your noses at all, do you?'

'What do you mean, "you people"?'

'Never mind. Come on.'

She winced at the mayhem ahead. The hum of the crowd was already making it difficult to talk. She considered girding her loins, but wasn't sure what it involved, so just got on with it instead and followed Tarkus into the tidal flow of the market. Within a moment they were surrounded by Night Folk, the next, by wonders. The Night Market contained every single thing for sale in this world and the next, and more besides. It was a heaving bedlam to which all of Midnight London had come to sell their wares, buy their shopping, or just for a good old gawk. Every single one of these people was shouting too, either to sell or to buy, or just to be heard. It was deafening.

'Two bats for a penny!'

'Fresh blood, who wants it fresh? You darlin'?'

'What'm I bid for a squid?'

There were sizzling greasy food stands wriggling with frying tentacles next to racks full of swan-feather cloaks, monster-sized eggs swaddled in straw rocked on warming tables next to huge plants with grabbing, reaching branches already full of stolen hats and wigs. There were badger-faced men with baskets full of snarling furballs, cage after cage of sweet-singing birds alongside death-screaming banshees, steins of grog whisked round on impossibly packed trays by hefty rhino-maidens, and other, weirder, things: a young girl with blue-tinged skin and all-black eyes speaking words that froze like ice in the air; an eight-armed man who pressed the foreheads of those who knelt before him, leaving a glowing mark. A flock of raven tailors draping shawls and dresses around customers in front of a brass mirror, and cawing viciously at any invasion of their space.

It was paralysing and fascinating and everywhere Emily's gaze fell there was more to wonder at. She blinked, and shook her head. How were they going to find modern tat in amongst every magic item and trinket in the world? She'd have to start asking people – if anyone would stand still long enough. Stallholders were mostly stuck in place, and might know about other market types. They struggled to the edges and started to wave her plastic lunchbox at people behind stands. She had two offers to buy it (one particularly insistent one from a man with shadows for eyes and a snake for a tongue), but was more generally ignored, shouted over or told to 'clear off from blocking the gentlefolk' (this from a man selling dung). It was all exhausting, not much fun, and was taking ages. There was only so long to go on her curfew timer too. She elbowed Tarkus in exasperation.

'We're never going to get round all this!' She had to stand close to him and shout because of the noise.

He pursed his lips. 'I hate to say it, but we'll have to split up. We can cover twice the ground.'

Emily's stomach lurched but . . .

'I suppose you're right.'

'I'll follow my nose and you do that thing you do where you wander straight into trouble face first.'

'Oi!' she said, but her heart wasn't in it. It was kind of true.

'Let's each do a big loop, then meet back by where we came in.' He rummaged in his coat and produced his large silver police whistle on a chain. He unclipped it and handed it to her.

'If you need me, then blow this and keep blowing it, and I'll come and find you. It's charmed, so I should be able to hear it over the crowd.'

'Brill!'

She grabbed it. She'd already got the end halfway to her mouth when his hand closed over hers.

'And *not* otherwise. You'll have every Night Watchman in the area here too, if you're not careful.'

'Spoilsport,' she said, but dropped the whistle inside her jacket pocket.

'Okay. Oh, also, standard Night Market rules apply, obviously.'

He turned to walk off.

'Eh, what rules?'

'Oh, you know, the usual ones,' he called over his shoulder. 'Don't make any promises, don't look at goblin men, don't proffer anything irreplaceable in payment and definitely don't eat any tasty looking fruit. Ha!'

'Wait, I can't remember all that.'

But he was gone with a wave.

'*Oh, you know, the usual ones,*' she said in her best Tarkus voice. 'Such a git.'

Where was she even supposed to start? She saw a gap in the crowd and made for it, and found there was only space because the Night Folk were leaving their usual superstitious distance around a dreamling – a human child whose sleeping mind had wandered into the Midnight Hour. He was silvery and see-through and not really there, all tousled hair and robot pyjamas, gawping with wonder at everything around him. What a crazy dream he must think he was having.

She'd never yet managed to talk to one and he looked oddly familiar, so she edged closer to see if she could say hello. She thought he saw her, but then a tribe of dancing lizards conga'd through the crowd, and the dreamling boy grinned madly and drifted sideways after them and was gone. Fair play, she'd much rather be doing that too.

After more fruitless searching, she was about to give up

when a fragrance on the edge of her senses caught her attention. There was a cacophony of smells here, but she had just smelt ... *Nah, couldn't be.* But, maybe Tarkus was right, and she should use her nose more? She'd got a half-Pooka schnozz after all. She inhaled deeply and gagged. *Blurgh; the land that soap forgot.* She wrinkled her nose, braced herself and tried again. Once she got through the very present odour of her fellow shoppers, there were other things – spices, the burnt ozone scent of magic and, and ... there it was. She would have sworn that was Chanel No. 5, her mum's favourite perfume, the one Emily sometimes sneakily dabbed on her wrists. She closed her eyes and inhaled more deeply, and again, turning around to follow the scent. It was coming through clearly now. It wasn't like any of the freaky scents in the Hour, it smelt of home and the real world. It was like her mum was right there. Thoughts of her mum evaporated with the jarring thud of her walking into somebody. Her heart gave a little skip, and she opened her eyes with a start to see only black. She looked up to find a tall lady in a black cloak with a hook nose, greenish skin and a significantly bristly chin looking down at her. She was wearing a pointy hat and carrying a broomstick. Emily didn't want to jump to conclusions but ...

'Did you just sniff me, morsel?' said the maybe-a-witch, glaring with a potentially evil eye.

'No! Well, yes, because of the smell.'

The probably-although-it-wasn't-fair-to-stereotype witch's eyes widened, and she started to twine her fingers together. A purple glow formed around her black nails.

'And by smell I mean the lovely lovely scent you are wearing,' Emily gabbled at a speed that might have broken the Guinness record for most words spoken in the shortest time. 'It is so so glorious and reminds me of the warm—darkest of nights and I would love to know where you got it from.'

Emily slowed down at the end as the might-just-be-a witch's expression had melted. Not melted like someone had thrown a bucket of water on her, but with a happy glow. The less happy glow around her fingers had thankfully gone out too. She smiled, revealing frankly disastrous dentistry.

'Well, curse you, that's so kind. I can't believe you noticed.'

Emily *could* believe she'd noticed, because now she was standing closer it became clear the whole 'less is more' thing hadn't been explained to the who-knows-possibly-just-a-misunderstood-old-herbalist, who absolutely reeked of what Emily was pretty sure was at least a bucketful of perfume.

'Oh, I've got a sensitive nose,' said Emily as she tried not to choke. 'Wherever did you get it from?'

'Why, from a little stall up the back there. A charming young man with many interesting things.'

She gestured vaguely behind her with her almost-certainly-only-used-for-cleaning broom.

'Brill,' said Emily. 'I'll head up there now.'

'Oh, that's a shame, I was about to invite you to tea. You seem such a sensitive young lady, and I have simply no one to talk to apart from my cat.'

Emily hesitated. It was difficult to leave when someone had done you a favour, and she didn't want to be judgy.

'I've got gingerbread,' said the green-skinned bakery connoisseur.

'Oh good lord, is that the time?' said Emily and strolled off sideways. 'Another day, I promise.'

'Oh,' said the disappointed cat owner. 'Well, of course, you must hop along. I'll hold you to that promise though.' She waved with the tips of her still faintly glowing fingers. 'I'm Ma Shipton, you can ask any of the necromantic community for me. Toodles!'

Emily hurriedly walked off, feeling bad that she may have been judgemental, then had to duck a minute later as a low-flying broom careened overhead, ridden manically by a figure in a black cloak who zapped a passing stall-holder into toad-dom, and flew off cackling madly.

'Total coincidence,' Emily said to herself, and carried on in her hunt for the stall.

Heading the way she'd been pointed, she started to spot more people with out-of-place (well, out-of-time was more accurate, she supposed) things in the crowd. A big pink handbag with a Gucci stamp carried by a muscly ogre, a *Walking Dead* T-shirt worn by a grinning zombie, and a hawk-faced man chewing a My Little Pony with great satisfaction. The crush of people pushed them past her before she could quiz them, but they'd all come from the same direction, so she kept on walking that way. Moments later, she spotted another clue and this one was standing still.

She forced her way out of the crowd and stopped right in front of a stall draped with heavily embroidered tapestries, run by a tall gobhoblin (like a hobgoblin, but much wider with weirder teeth according to her mum). His ample frame was draped in a velvet kaftan, and he wore an unusual piece of red headgear. He seemed disconcerted to have a small human tugging at his voluminous sleeve, but it might just have been his teeth.

'Mate, excuse me, but, wow, I've always wanted to say this.' Emily pointed up. 'Where did you get that hat?'

She coughed but couldn't resist.

'Where *did* you get that hat?'

'Ahhh, you noticed!' The gobhoblin smiled with pleasure, and reached for the long brow and pulled it from his head, revealing two little horns, and a small snoozy sparrow asleep in a nest of oily hair underneath.

'Most excellent, isn't it? The latest fashion, the milliner told me. My tiny bird is most delighted.'

He held the hat up and admired it. It had a rounded headpiece, like half a ball, with a strap for adjustment at the rear, and at the front a protruding beak to shade the wearer's eyes.

'Yeah, it's brill. Where did you get it?'

'Why, from a wonderful new stall. Just up the top there, on the left, you can't miss it.' He pointed it out.

'Nice one. In return, two bits of advice on the hat front. One, this is actually called a baseball cap.' She tapped it with her finger. 'Two, it's like twice as fashionable if you wear it backwards.' She spun it in his hands and lifted it up. The gobhoblin popped it back on his head, over the still snoozing sparrow, and adjusted the brim at the rear.

'Like this?'

'Oh yeah. Totally radical,' she said, and somehow, despite all the odds, managed to keep a straight face. The gobhoblin beamed and bowed. Behind him, the tapestries hung on the stall caught her eye. They were intricately embroidered with scenes showing the glorious past of the Night Folk; elf queens and vampire knights, cheerful werewolves swallowing the evil Day Folk. But these were different than normal tapestries, because they swarmed with movement. Knights and queens stopped their busy work of eating the poor and preying on the unwary, and all turned to face her. The stitches rippled as they moved.

'Oh, that's cool,' she said to the gobhoblin, but he only hissed in reply. His lips had slid back to show more curly teeth as he stared at the tapestries. An anxious tweeting came from beneath his cap, and he backed away from his own stall. Her Pooka danger sense flared up with a hot flush behind her ears. The figures in the tapestries loomed larger now, drawn closer to the front of the material and peering out as through a window. They were all staring straight at her too. The figures at the front, the knight and the elf queen, grasped for her. Their hands tented out the tapestries they hung in, and their faces distorted with silent anguish.

By this point, Emily was already on her toes and gone. 'Nope nope nopey nope nope,' she muttered as she hurtled away past the gobhoblin whose cap was tweeting and trying to take off. An icy chill gripped her. They definitely weren't meant to do that. The gobhoblin had looked horrified. The worst part was that she had seen the exact same thing once tonight already. The statue in the park. The figures in the tapestry had acted exactly like the statue. What on earth was going on?

She slowed and walked on blindly, her head full of whatever it was that had just happened. She soon came to a point where the crowd had thickened so much she couldn't get through. A bottleneck had formed at one stand as folk clustered around it, blocking the way. All of a sudden, the tapestries were forgotten. She squirmed her way to the front by deploying pointy elbows, standing on toes and leaving a trail of muttering behind her.

The stall was little more than a suitcase on a plank, but it was full of jumbled, brightly coloured wonders that seemed as alien in this place as magic would in a maths class at home. The suitcase brimmed with the gaudiest of tat – Spice Girls mugs, royal wedding T-shirts and tattered London Eye postcards. It was a terrible gallimaufry of naffness that would have embarrassed the worst of boot sales, and it was all from her world. This was it – the source of the magic leak.

She stepped up to the stall at the same moment as the stallholder straightened up from underneath it, holding a lava lamp. Their eyes met and they both froze.

'Jaysus,' said Uncle Pat.

CHAPTER 6

'**Y**ou!' said Emily. She was too shocked to shout. Her stomach clenched while her hands knotted into fists.

'Are ye sure?' asked Pat in his broad Irish accent. He had a faded tweed jacket on that couldn't even have been described kindly as shabby, a black flat cap and a red scarf. 'I mean I could be somebody else; I do look a lot like another fella. He's a right one by all accounts.' He winked at the crowd over her head, and there was a ripple of laughter.

'Oh it's definitely you, all right,' said Emily through gritted teeth. 'I don't forget people who lie and cheat and nearly cause the whole world to end!'

'That does sound like the other fella,' Pat mused.

'There is no other fella, Pat!' she shouted. 'It was you. It *is* you. You caused the whole thing in the first place and then you locked me out and then . . .' She'd run out of breath and was just inhaling to start again when he interrupted.

'And was it not fine?'

'What?'

'Was it not fine? Did it not, in fact, turn out all right in the end, the world being saved, evil defeated and all was well and such?' He grinned. 'Was that not in fact what happened?'

'Well, yes, I guess. But that's not the point! You nearly—'

'Ahh, nearly nothing. I said catemegorical like it would all be fine, and –' he raised a finger to illustrate his point, paused while it was up there and extracted a rolled-up cigarette from behind his ear – 'it was. Grand, so. I was right all along, and there's no cause for all yer carrying on here.'

Emily was thunderstruck by the immense wrongness of his viewpoint. The worst bit was that she didn't have any good argument against it.

'You! *You* . . . It's that type of thinking . . .'

'Aye?' He cocked his head on one side, waiting.

'Argh!' She kicked the stand, causing him to clutch at the wobbling suitcase precariously balanced on the plank. 'You're a terrible, terrible man and I really don't like you!'

'Ahh, you sound just like me dear old mammy.' His grin widened. 'Now, can you hop out the way – ye're playing murder with me passing trade.'

There were rumblings in the crowd around her but the burning iron of Emily's rage became focused into one needle-sharp point, and she grinned right back at him.

'Oh well, Patrick, it's this "trade" of yours I'd like to discuss. I am on official business from the Library.' She whipped out her Library card and held it up over her head for all to see. 'Official business as a detective with the Night Watch to find out who is illegally bringing in things from the Daylight.'

He didn't answer, but his eyes narrowed with suspicion like a squinting snake. The crush of people around Emily melted away. The crowd had suddenly remembered other important things they should be doing and were all leaving. She whipped up her hand into a finger gun and fired it in his face. 'Which I just did. It's *you*!'

To his credit, he didn't even flinch. He waved the roll-up-holding hand at her to clear away the fog of false accusations, leaving a trail of dirty smoke in its path.

'Ah, that'll be the deceptiveness of the old appearances there. What it actually is was, I was happening by this stall, when the owner, great big tall fella, all over with the hair and stuff –' his hand sketched this statuesque hirsute retail proprietor for her – 'he asked as on account of me appearing honest and such, whether I'd mind the spot while he went to the lavvy.' He nodded sagely at his own story. 'He's been a while, mind. I guess it must be murder going to the lav with all that dangling hair—'

'Stop!' Emily shouted, not wishing to deal with that mental image. 'So it's nothing to do with you at all? It's some hairy bloke?'

He looked her straight in the eye, and spoke clearly and without hesitation. The FBI would have believed him. A lie detector would not have even pinged.

'Exactly. Never seen any of it before ten minutes ago. It's the strangest coincidence really, niece of mine.'

'Right,' said Emily, looking him up and down. 'As strange a coincidence as you wearing jeans, trainers and a SpongeBob T-shirt?

He looked down, silent for a moment.

'Advertising?' he tried. Even he didn't sound convinced.

'Pat! This is serious. I don't care if it's dodgy, I just need to know how it got here.'

He folded his arms across his chest and shook his head. 'I never reveals me sources. It goes against the founding principles of free trade and investigative journalling.'

'You haven't got any principles!' she said.

He actually looked affronted.

'That I do, but they're . . . situational. This is one of those situations.'

'Look, this stuff –' Emily whacked the suitcase, making a furry gonk fall off the end of a bright pink pencil – 'is coming through a rip in the spell. And every time it's used, it makes it worse. It's dangerous and it's damaging the whole Hour. The *whole Hour*, Pat.'

'The Hole?' He gave a guilty jerk. 'What Hole? I wouldn't know anything about a Hole now. What's it even look like? You've got the wrong fella.'

Emily stared meaningfully at him while he twitched.

'Pat, I didn't mention "a hole" or "the hole" or anything. I said "rip" before.'

'Did I say "Hole"? I meant . . . ho well? You weren't listening fast enough.'

Pat had an itch under his cap and he scratched it while he talked. Emily was certain now.

'Tell me about the Hole, Patrick, or I swear I will wreak a terrible vengeance on you and your shins.'

He bit his lip until it went white, his roll-up crushed between his tightened fingers. He didn't look at her as he spoke.

'Maybe if there was a Hole, all hypothetical now, and it was getting a lot of use say, on the old import/export front, would that be bad then?'

'Yes! Really bad. It could destroy everything. Tell me, Pat, where is it?'

He mulled. The internal conflict was obvious as his lips

twitched against each other like wrestling caterpillars. He was about to speak when he looked over her shoulder. His eyes went wide and his face rigid with shock.

'Oh jaysus, is the Library herself coming now too?'

Emily spun around to look. Bookface would make this a lot easier. She craned her neck but there was no sign of her in the crowd.

'Where?' she said, turning back to Pat. Who wasn't there either, and nor was his suitcase. Because she was an idiot who had fallen for 'look behind you'. *Damn it!* Never trust a Pooka.

She grabbed the whistle out of her jacket and let rip with a long, clear blast that cut silver through the night. The crowd froze for a second, and she caught a glimpse of a black-jacketed figure in blue jeans sprinting into the distance with a suitcase.

She blew another loud, shrill blast as shoppers around her covered their ears, then put her head down and ran after her uncle. Tarkus would just have to catch up.

She pounded into the night. The market and its lights receded behind her and she was running through streets lit first by the occasional gas lamp and then only the silver of the moon. Pat was already far in the distance – god, he was fast for a man who smoked as much as he did. She was panting like a smoker herself as she ran after him, but there was no way she was letting him disappear. He was jinking down lanes in a bid to throw her off his trail but her Pooka senses were tingling on high alert and she could half smell and half feel where he'd gone. It also helped that he hadn't closed the suitcase properly. Plastic flamingos and biros had spilt on to the ground and now guided her along.

She rounded a corner and found the suitcase cast aside, with plastic tat spilling around it like an art installation. Beyond it, a disreputable-looking black hound was haring it down the street. She caught a glimpse of his gleaming red eyes and a pink tongue lolling out of a grinning mouth as he glanced back at her. His four feet were faster than the previous two, and he hurtled off ahead of her.

Emily didn't stop. She hurdled the suitcase and kept on going. He wasn't going to get away. She reached for her hare shape, then hesitated. She couldn't change with the Hog in her pocket, and was already wiped out from her earlier failure. She'd have to do it the old-fashioned way. She focused on the pain of when he tricked and abandoned her, and let her deep inner need to really shout at him fuel her. Never underestimate the power of anger. She put her head down and threw herself down the street behind him.

After endless sweaty minutes, she barrelled out into a wide empty area of scrub ground in the shadow of the vast arch of a railway bridge. There was Pooka scent here but she couldn't tell which way Pat had gone. The instant she stopped, her lungs put their foot down. She was out of air, and had to lean forward, arms on thighs, and try to both breathe and not throw up at the same time. She had a stitch and her calves throbbed and—

She spotted a set of red eyes gleaming in the darkness of the railway arch and all her pain was forgotten.

'Patrick, come on! I just want to talk.'

She limped towards him, then stopped as he padded out of the shadow into the moonlight. He was bigger and sleeker now, not half as disreputable, and much more dangerous looking. He was giving her a distinctly funny look, and snarling.

'Damn it, Pat, what are you doing—'

The sleek and dangerous-looking dog gave a flicker of black light and, with the hiss of an angry cobra, expanded out into a sleek and dangerous-looking girl. She was striking, with long red hair, green eyes, and the same vicious snarl on her face that the dog had worn. The girl probably wasn't more than a couple of years older than Emily, but in a black velvet cobwebbed top and slinky leather trousers she held herself like a different, more regal, species. She looked Emily up and down, and sneered.

'Whuh?' said Emily. That wasn't Pat. He couldn't have pulled those trousers off for starters. Behind slinky snarly girl, another set of red eyes blinked into view in the darkness, then another and another until Emily couldn't keep count. They all flowed around her, splitting left and right, and the darkness filled with them as they encircled Emily. Set after set of glaring, glowing red eyes on huge black dogs.

'Ah,' Emily said.

None of them looked much like Pat's dog form. They were bigger, sharper, altogether scarier looking. Pat had always looked impressive as a hound (if terribly annoying in person) but he was potentially the runt of the litter, it seemed. The pack speeded up and circled around her in an unnerving silence. As they grew faster their red eyes began to blur into a single red line. They were a whirlwind of black silk with red flames streaking it.

She turned this way and that, head reeling as the hounds circled. The red-headed girl flashed a knife of a grin and pointed at her. As she did, the pack came to a dead halt. All eyes were on Emily.

'And what do we have here? It doesn't smell right, whatever it is,' said the girl.

This was clearly not going to go well.

'Look,' began Emily, holding up her hands in the universal gesture of, *I'd really rather this didn't turn nasty.* 'I'm just trying to track down Unc— Patrick Connolly. He's Pooka, like you. Like me,' she said, quietly at the end.

The girl's knife smile grew even sharper.

'Like ye? Like ye? There's no Pooka like ye, daysie girl!'

She was speaking to the crowd as much as she was speaking to Emily. There was a ripple of growls and wheezing, the doggy version of laughter. In the years before Emily had developed the mechanism of the gob to scare off bullies, she had met people like this at school.

'I don't want any trouble, I'm just—'

She didn't get any further. The girl had crossed the distance between them in a blink of Pooka speed, and was now right in her face.

'Oh, but trouble ye've found.' Her eyes were bright green, and her grin had nothing kind in it at all.

Emily wasn't sure what would have happened next if a rather dodgy black-but-shabby hound hadn't squeezed out of the pack, and pushed in between Emily and the girl. It rubbed against their legs, pushing the girl back a step or two, then twined round behind Emily. With a hand-dryer whoosh of displaced air, Pat stood at her side, hand ever so gently on her shoulder.

'Well this is a turn-up, eh? A happy family reunion.'

The girl snarled again. 'I should have known.'

Pat smiled as if she hadn't spoken. 'Niece, meet our dearest cousin, Bronagh, daughter of Great-Auntie Aoife (may she rest in pieces). Bron, meet your third cousin, Emily, daughter of—'

Bronagh cut him off, her face rippled with disgust. 'I

can smell whose and what she is. Daysie. Half-breed. Traitor's daughter.'

Emily had already had enough of Bron, cousin or not, and now the fierce and virtuous light of anger filled her like a power station turning on. The gob was raring to go.

'Right, look, dog-breath, you don't know me from Pedigree Chum, but if you say one more word about my mum—'

Bronagh closed the gap between them again in a blink, and glared into Emily's eyes. Bronagh's own eyes flashed crimson, and her face flickered back and forth to that of an enormous wolf-like dog. *Oh wow, she might even be angrier than me*, thought Emily.

'Ye'll what?'

Emily gulped, the gob being edged out by sudden fear.

'I'll be really, really cross?' she said. 'I'll probably say something terribly cutting too, and you'll feel bad about yourself for days afterwards.'

Bronagh snarled and gave her a shove. She was slight but seriously strong, and Emily staggered back.

'Another joker.' Bron shoved her again, harder this time. 'Another fool.'

'Whoa there, ladies,' yelled Pat, spiralling on one heel and sliding in between them again, like a dancer. He had, thought Emily with one of those weird blurts that filled her brain whenever things turned nasty, missed out on a whole alternate career on *Strictly*. 'There's no need for that, Bron, she's family.'

'She's a mongrel from the worst litter this clan's ever thrown is what she is,' Bron snapped back at him. 'Should have been drowned in a barrel and saved us all the problem. Sure and I might do it now.'

She was snarling, her eyes awash with scarlet fury. Her teeth were definitely more canine than human now.

'That's fierce unkind of ye now, Bronagh,' said Pat.

Despite the fear that rippled through Emily's tummy, something about Bron just riled her. It might have been the perfect hair. Or the death threats. Before she knew it, the gob had slipped its leash again.

'I'm not being lectured on breeding by a gothic show-poodle.' She could hear her mouth motoring but couldn't stop the words. 'Go buy a flea comb and we'll talk.'

Bron barked with rage. She flew at Emily even as Pat grabbed at her shoulder to try and stop her. They hit the floor together as Bron's weight carried them over. Emily closed her eyes and curled down behind her hands, as Bron clawed for her throat.

'Ye're dead!' Bron snarled.

CHAPTER 7

'*That's enough of that now!*'

The voice was dry and old but cut clearly through the crowd, and echoed under the railway arch.

Bronagh snarled at the sound of it and pulled Emily right up to her face, holding her bomber jacket with white-knuckled fists.

'Bronagh! Don't test me.' The whip-crack voice again.

Bron's whole face contorted and her eyes flared red like a nuclear sunset, but she dumped Emily back to the ground and stepped away. Emily gasped for breath as she yanked her jacket back down, and scrabbled to her feet. Pat leant to whisper in her ear.

'Look, if ye're wanting to be finding out more about the old aitch oh ell ee, then this is the place. Don't say yer old Uncle Pat never does ye a favour, eh?'

'You call this a favour!' she whispered back furiously. He winked at her. Before she could strangle him, the voice came again.

'Now, what in the name of Danu goes on here?'

Emily looked to see who had saved her from needing dental surgery (and possibly rabies shots). Many of the Pooka had shifted back into human form, and there were a lot of rangy, disreputable-looking types standing around, with a mix of long dark hair and red curly locks, apparently competing for who could look the most dodgy. There was a lot of black velvet and glossy leather and very few smiles. Striding through the middle of this pack was an old woman. She had thick white hair, a face furrowed with lines, a black patch over one eye, and a thick floor-length fur coat with a massive collar. She looked deeply grumpy, somewhat piratical, and definitely regal. There was no doubt who was in charge here, even before the rest of the clan dipped their heads to her. Even Pat took his cap off. Emily realized that, if she squinted and half closed her eyes, the ferocious old lady looked a lot like her mum.

Oh.

Pat nudged her, and used his quite-loud stage whisper again.

'This is Mammy Espeth. She's mine and your ma's ma, which makes her yer—'

'Yes, I know how it works.'

Emily had a deep gurgling discomfort in her tummy. She'd wanted to meet her family for years, but Mammy didn't look much happier to see her than Bronagh had.

'I said, what in the very devil is going on here?' said Mammy.

Pat winked at Emily, switched on a megawatt smile and stepped forward with his arms held wide.

'If it's not my dear old mammy. I'm home again. Kill the fatted calf, eh?'

'Don't "mammy" me, ye feckless halfwit,' said the old lady.

Pat beamed even more. 'Ahh, it's like I never left. Mammy, this is—'

'I can smell who she is, Patrick. What possessed you to bring her here to the gathering?'

The old lady was ignoring Emily as if she wasn't there. Bron was grinning at this snub, and Emily's anger boiled back up.

'Now, Mammy, there's things ye should know—' began Pat, but the old lady silenced him with a glare. She swished her coat, releasing a cloud of a thick tobacco scent, and paced in front of the crowd.

'Pooka are blessed with many offspring normally.' She

rubbed her bristly chin as she paced, head shaking slowly. 'Just two I had, and fallen far they both have from the tree.'

The shock of recognition caught Emily by surprise. She knew what this was. It was the start of a dramatic monologue, exactly like the ones her mum did about the neighbour she was feuding with. If she'd had any doubts they were related, they'd just disappeared. This *was* her nan.

'Just two,' Mammy continued, 'one an idiot, one a traitor.'

'OI!' snapped Emily and Pat, both at the same time. Mammy took no notice, deep in her tragic speech now.

'It is kings we are descended from, *kings*, and yet now reduced to jesters.' She shot Pat a particularly sharp glance at this point. 'It weighs heavy upon me.'

There was a sympathetic rumble from the surrounding Pooka.

Emily had a lot of experience of this type of public proclaiming. When her mum did it, she would get progressively more worked up, like a washing machine going through its program. Emily estimated that Mammy was on 'rinse' currently, and if she got to 'spin' they could be here for a while. She jumped into the dramatic pause.

'My mum's not a traitor.' She didn't say it with anger, just loudly and clearly. 'She's saved the Midnight world, *your world*, twice now.'

A whisper and a rustle went up from the surrounding Pooka.

Who's she think she is? Like we even needed savin'.

Mammy finally deigned to look at her, and gave her an icy glare.

'We do not speak of her.'

'You just did!'

More rumblings from the chorus.

Ah, she's got her there.

Mammy's brow creased, and her eye flickered red.

'Look, I don't want to get into an argument. I'm not even supposed to be here or talking to you at all,' said Emily.

An *ooh* from the chorus.

She thinks she's better than we are.

'Look, I just need one thing and I'll go. The Library—'

There was a collective groaning shudder.

The big scary book lady . . .

'The Library wants to know where the tear—' She used the name Pat had dropped instead. '—The Hole is. I know you know where it is. Tell me where the Hole is and I'll go.'

A silence full of whispers and elbowing from the chorus. *She knows we know she knows.*

Emily would have sworn Mammy's gaze had briefly flitted to Bron when she'd mentioned the Hole. Other than that, Mammy's face was expressionless, not even a flicker to show she cared or was interested.

'Please. It's letting magic pour out. If it's not closed, it'll be a disaster for everyone in here, including you.'

Mammy dug inside her coat and pulled out a long, thin black pipe. She tamped the end then clicked her long fingernails together to produce a flame as red as her eyes. She lit the pipe and puffed out a cloud of thick green smoke, and said nothing.

'Please listen, it's really mega important; the Library was super serious about the whole thing. It could break the Midnight Hour.'

Mammy's eyes widened just fractionally and she was about to speak when Bron did instead.

'And if it does? If this whole Hour crumbled, we'd no more be prisoners in here.' She held her hands out like a preacher delivering a prophecy. 'Since the Library shut the doors on us, the Hole's been our only way out. Imagine if it freed us completely! To run wild again in our power, bringing devilment to the daysies.'

There was a distinct uptick in the Pooka chorus; mostly mutterings of approval.

Now that's a point she's got, eh?

'We are ill-omen made flesh, and once we brought despair in our wake. It can be that way again!'

'Oh, you must be fun at parties,' muttered Emily, who was genetically incapable of keeping her gob shut. The red-haired girl whirled round to glare at her, and Mammy twisted her lip in what was nearly a smile. The old woman tugged at her pipe, then spat on the floor.

'Perhaps there's something in the child's warning—'

Before Mammy could go any further, there was a screech from behind her.

'NO! We've been trapped too long!' snarled Bronagh. 'The Hole is a blessing. She's not part of the clan! She's exiled, a traitor! You heard her, working for the Library. I say we—'

'YOU SAY NOTHING!' The volume of the roar was unexpected coming from the mouth of the old lady. Her face was pale with rage. 'I don't remember dying and making you clan chief.'

'But—' began Bron.

'Oh wait, let me check,' said Mammy, talking over her. She held a hand to her heart in a pantomime gesture. 'No, still beating, which means I'm still *in charge*.'

(It was at this point Emily decided she could probably get to like Mammy, if it wasn't for the whole 'exiled' thing.)

'But—' said Bron again, but Mammy ploughed on.

'Unless you want to challenge me, Bronagh? Is that how it goes?' She gestured around. 'We're gathered as a clan, ye have the right.'

There was a collective gasp and every Pooka leant in.

Bron's head snapped up and her eyes glowed red. She was definitely thinking about it. She took a step forward and flexed her fingers out like claws, but then her eyes twitched to the side. She was looking at the shadow cast by Mammy. The old lady hadn't moved in the slightest, just stood there with her arms folded. The moon cast a distinct hard-edged shadow at her side though, and this shadow had started to move. It grew and roiled and bloated out to five times the size of the old lady, filling out into a mass with four legs and the bulk of a rhino. The shadow solidified into one that would be cast by a giant and awful hound, its fang-filled mouth open and dripping.

The crowd of Pooka murmured and shuffled back, shaping themselves to be generally more behind Mammy Espeth and less behind Bron, so as not to give the wrong impression. Bronagh's gaze flickered between the shadow and the old lady, caught in a vice.

'Well?' said Mammy, and it was her voice but also a terrible subsonic growl that buzzed up through Emily's feet. Bron's face paled, and she took a half-step back and ducked her head in submission.

'As you say, Mammy. It shall be as you say.'

'Of course it will,' said the old lady, and puffed at her filthy pipe.

Pat elbowed Emily in the side again.

'Do *not* mess with Mammy,' he whispered with a grin. Bron shot them both a murderous look and retreated. The Pooka all stood away from her, just to be on the safe side.

'I'll say it again – maybe the child has a point.' Mammy wrinkled her nose up. 'The Hole's a rough piece of magic and no mistake.'

Emily's heart leapt.

'But my snarling niece has a point too,' said Mammy and she turned to address Emily directly now, and Emily's heart sank. 'Ye can't just storm into a gathering of the clan and ask for help without proving yerself a part of us.'

There was a big huff of nudging and pointing from the crowd.

The test! The test!

'Prove yerself Pooka, and maybe we'll make an arrangement,' the old lady said, then continued in a voice barely more than a whisper. 'She'll have taught you that much at least, right?'

This was the first time Mammy had given the slightest indication she acknowledged who Emily was to her, and Emily flushed with warmth despite herself. It was soon swamped with cold worry about what she was being asked to do though.

'Erm, what?' She looked at Pat and he shrugged.

'She means show yer power. Just some basic Pooka-ing; change form, push yer luck, commit glorious trickery, that kind of thing.' He smiled encouragingly. 'Just do one.'

'Oh right, like in front of everybody? Now?' said Emily.

The gaze of all the Pooka was now solidly on her again,

including the furious green of Bronagh's and the single beady black glare of Mammy. The chorus had stopped murmuring, which was even more unnerving.

Emily's heart iced up, her stomach flipped and rolled, and she had a serious need to go for a wee. This was even worse than auditioning for the school play when she'd totally frozen up and ended up throwing the script into the front row and getting stuck in a curtain as she'd run off stage. She could still taste the velvet.

'Well?' said Mammy. Emily had started to think she might have been on her side, but her gaze was unforgiving and her face was stone. 'Can yer?'

'Erm. Yes, sure. I can do the hare, I might just need somebody to shout "boo".' She winced as a ripple of laughter passed through the crowd.

The hare she said, the hare!

Mammy shook her head.

'Hare is the child's form. There's not a Pooka here couldn't do it in the cradle. Will you suck your thumb for us too?'

Laughter went through the crowd as the Pooka elbowed each other. It came loudest from Bronagh.

Emily stared at her boots. Pat took her elbow and stage whispered, 'You need to do the hound. Come on, ye've got this. It'll be a breeze.'

'Oh god, really?' Her stomach was full of rocks and her

head was way too heavy to hold up. She also hoped dogs' bladders weren't much smaller or she was going to wet herself even if she did manage it. She gritted her teeth, and tried to give it the all-important 'of course I've done the revision' confidence.

'Right, you should have said. No bother.' She waved a casual hand and hoped no one saw it shaking. 'I do this all the time. Big fan of sniffing bums and peeing up lamp posts me.'

Why did she have to mention peeing? She handed her backpack and jacket to Pat, as the Hog would never forgive her for changing with him onboard, then faced the crowd.

She took a deep breath, closed her eyes, thought about how horribly scared she was, and how much she'd love to run away. She took that feeling and rolled it up in her head into a crackling ball of energy, and, clenching her fist, crushed it and pulled it inward. The energy of it started to flow into the other place inside her, where the magic was, and her other shapes that waited there stirred in their sleep. Her energy wanted to flow into the wrapper that was her hare shape, wanted to fuel long legs and ears and the familiar shrinking feeling, but she mastered it and moved beyond it and, groping in the dark, reached for the hound again.

She found thick fur, and muscled flank, and sharp teeth and sensitive nose. She grasped it where she'd missed it before so many times, and pulled herself in with a shock of the new and with an electric thrill at the fact she was really doing this. She was putting the magic jumper on! She didn't panic, but instead breathed herself out into this new space, filled up the shape from the inside, as her outside was shrinking, as she landed on to four solid feet and . . . she was back in the night with a new form and a nose that could smell the whole world.

A million odours poured in through that nose: the street, the pack around her, a whole other sensory realm she hadn't known was there. That was how she knew she had done it. She had done it!

So why was Pat looking down at her in horror?

CHAPTER 8

She looked up at Pat, for he was above her now, a long way above her in fact. He was biting his knuckle, eyes wide. Her ears, so sensitive now, pricked up, and all she heard was laughter, gales of laughter. She whirled back around (as a tail whipped away behind her that she had the urge to chase) and Mammy Espeth stared down at her with a grim expression. The old woman didn't say a thing, just shook her head and walked away.

'What?' Emily tried to say and barked instead. Not a terrifying wolf-like bark either, more of a yip. Behind Pat the assembled Pooka looked like they'd been hit by a bowling ball. They were staggering, or on their knees, clutching each other and all howling with laughter. One was crying and another was laughing so hard he was nearly sick. In the midst of them all was Bronagh, pointing at Emily with fierce triumph in her eyes and cackling fit to burst.

It must have gone wrong, but Emily didn't know how. She jigged one way then the other, but it was difficult to see yourself when you were a dog. There was a furry flank, and back legs (which did look a bit short, come to mention it) and that tantalizing tail, but she couldn't *see*. She bounded, well, scurried, away to the side of the scrub ground and found a big puddle. She resisted the urge to lap at it, and stared down at herself.

What stared back was not a red-eyed, black-furred hell-hound. It wasn't even black, let alone hellish. It was instead a short-legged, grey-furred, terrier-looking, somewhat podgy mix-up of a scruffy mongrel. She was a red lead and a tartan coat away from being an old lady's dog. She wasn't a hound, she was a pooch, a failure, and not a proper Pooka at all.

Obviously she ran away. It was one of her go-to coping mechanisms and she was even more genetically inclined to do so as a terrier. She legged it, with the howling laughter of her so-called family echoing in her ears and burning a place in her soul. She ran, all four of her legs churning away, bum jiggling and tail waggling, under the railway arch and away from the pain, even as she carried it with her. She knew, in the instant of it happening, that she would be dreaming and daydreaming about this utter humiliation for her whole life. It would pop up on quiet afternoons or otherwise nice days for years to come and whisper in her ear – *oh hey, remember the time when your whole world collapsed into shame denser than a black hole?* – and make her stomach clench so tight she'd groan aloud. That was how it was going to be.

She ran, and panted, and her big pink tongue lolled out as she did. The smells of the night poured in. Her dog nose was far more sensitive than her hare nose. She could smell everything: the trails of other Pooka who had run through here, and everyone else who'd come up or down this lane today. They were in her head, layer after layer of different coloured threads, each streaming away at a different pace: there a troll who stomped by in the morning; there the rich but separated scent of a hopping Chinese vampire; all of them telling her their story at the slightest sniff. It was like being given a whole extra pair of eyes that could see around corners and back in time. It was magical and brilliant and she didn't give a monkey's. She was filled only with teeth-clenching embarrassment and shame as she chumbled along, her waggly back end jinking out side to side as she travelled over the uneven cobbles. She'd even got a stupid walk. Her small doggy mind wasn't big enough for the thoughts she was having, and she wanted to get out of this ridiculous shape. First, however . . . she checked both sides of the street, found a handy gas lamp and had one of the more satisfying wees of her life.

She waddled further up the street away from her puddle and let the rubber band of the change energy pull her back into herself with the *swoooff* of a big feather pillow being flattened. She staggered as she went back to two legs, and the after-effect of the change hit her straight away. She clutched on to a nearby wall, unable to go any further. Then, naturally, she cried.

After she'd got that over with, she hunched down on a doorstep and pulled the silver whistle out of her jeans pocket. She started blowing it at regular, ear-piercing intervals and hoped Tarkus would be able to find her. After five minutes or so, instead of the floral scent she'd hoped for there was a familiar waft of tobacco instead, and a distinct medicinal smell she had long suspected wasn't medicine at all. Pat was meandering down the street towards her. He had his fingers jammed in his ears.

'Jeez, would ye put a sock in it? Ye're the wrong end of town to be hoping for the Watch, girl.'

She put her head down and blew the whistle harder, then ran out of puff. The whistle trailed off with a sad silvery burble.

He sidled over. She didn't look up. His trainers were ridiculous: all bright and yellow and wrong against the moonlit cobbles.

'Well, ye've got the running away thing down anyways. Key Pooka skill that.'

'Go away! I hate you,' she said.

'Ye sound more like yer mam every day, ye know.'

Pat stood in front of her and held out her backpack and her jacket. She clutched at them. In her shame she hadn't realized she'd left them behind. She was sure that the Hog would be gone because that was what she deserved, but as she lifted the jacket up the buzzing sound of little snores drifted out. She breathed a sigh of relief and caught Pat's eye, and he smiled that wry half-smile of his. That smile, she thought, was the honest one, not the big beaming fake one he was so good at.

'His lordship's fine, don't worry yerself. Now budge up.'

She didn't, but he jammed himself in next to her on the doorstep anyway. He leant an elbow on one knee.

'Look, it's not as bad as ye think.'

'Really?' said Emily. 'Because I couldn't have imagined that happening in my worst nightmares. Even the ones where I'm chased by a bear.' She shivered as she remembered the laughter echoing around her. The look on Mammy's face as she walked away was worse.

'I'll never get to . . .' She didn't even know what she wouldn't get: a nan, a family, some kind of Pooka clan badge? Just that she'd blown it in a horribly public way.

Pat shook his head.

'I'm telling ye, it's okay. We've all got different other forms. A lot of it's how ye see yerself.'

'I see myself as a fat terrier?' Emily glared at him. 'Please stop trying to help.'

He sighed. 'Look, ye saw Bronagh's hound self, right?'

A sharp black blade in dog form. 'Yeah, she's scary.'

'Aye. She's so all over on being "dark" that it comes out in hers. Now think of my own fine shape.'

She squinted. 'Dog-you looks . . . dodgy.'

''Xactly!' He slapped his knee and grinned. 'Ye saw Mammy's shadow too, didn't ye?'

The shadow that had grown and grown beneath the moon. Emily shivered and Pat nodded.

'Even more 'xactly. That's sheer power and will, and a streak of turrible temper right there.'

'So what are you saying?'

'I'm saying maybe the wee dog is just more . . . ye.' He settled back against the door, and didn't meet her eye. 'Maybe ye're not all bite like ye sound.'

She slumped forward and rested her head on her hands.

'You mean it shows my inner failure. Great.'

'No! I mean, ah jaysus, this really isn't my line.' He was scratching under his cap as he spoke. 'I mean that maybe ye're a bit less confident than ye make out, or summat, and it's okay or whatever it is.' He started to make a horrid-smelling cigarette so he had somewhere else to look.

'I'm not sure this is helping,' she said.

'I'm not sure either. I'm not qualified for this. D'yer want a ciggie?'

'*No!*'

He lit the horrible roll-up from a sulphurous smelling match and she jumped off the step to get away from the pungent stink of smoke.

'Look, we're all different,' he said.

'Oh please.' Emily rolled her eyes.

He waved her quiet with his smoking hand, weaving a red zigzag in the air.

'No, I mean Pooka. We've all got different erm . . . faucets.'

He folded his thumb and little finger to touch tips across his palm and held up the three remaining fingers to her. It had the practised motion of a ritual.

'We possess the blessing of triple form. We're all different in that and it changes as we grow. Yer hare's good, right?'

'I suppose,' she said, staring at her boots. 'When I can get it to work.'

'Well, yer hound will get better too, if you can find the right kick up the jacksy. Yer horse might be great an' all.' He spun a finger in a circle to show the whole Pooka world. 'We're all different. Same as with the pushing yer luck stuff, and—'

Emily stopped staring at her boots. 'What luck stuff? Like being able to hold the bad pennies?'

Emily had been able to carry her mum's dramatically cursed coin necklace without a problem, while just touching them had put a number of other people into casualty, one via a rhino. The bad luck they carried didn't affect Pooka, because they were creatures of 'bad luck and ill-omen' themselves.

'Maeve hasn't taught ye anything, has she?' He frowned as he tugged on his vile roll-up. 'We can push our luck; that's the other part of the blessing.'

'Eh?' Emily squinted through the pulse of a deep and growing headache. This often happened in conversations with Pat.

'Push our luck.' Pat thrust his arm out before him, his nicotine-stained hand flat to push invisible luck.

'We can get rid of the bad luck on to people . . .' He pulled his closed hand back towards him. ' . . . and take the good. It's why people are thinking we're unlucky, right.'

'Because you literally steal their good luck? That is—'

'Ahh, details, details,' said Pat, waving away whatever she'd been about to say. 'Anyway, we're not talking about luck. We're talking about that red-haired mare, Bron.'

Emily's headache pulsed as she tried to follow him.

'I thought we were talking about me being a podgy doggy?'

'Ahh, it's all related. Just like our lot.' He grinned and hopped up from the step to stand in front of her.

'Our Bron's not been the same since her ma died. The joy's gone out of her and she's all about this ill-omen and getting out the Hour. She thinks we're prisoners.'

'But Mammy doesn't think that, does she?'

Emily flinched as she said the name. She'd finally met her mysterious nan, and it had been awful.

'I'm not sure where she's at. She's been in a fierce dark mood since the War and her exiling Maeve and all.' He sighed. 'She's not the ma as used to take us chicken scrumping, I know that. She broods a lot, and Bronagh's been getting ideas about who should be in charge.'

'Pat,' said Emily, 'this is all, just for once, actually fascinating, but what on earth has it got to do with me?'

He looked at her as if she'd turned green.

'Because of the Hole, y'eejit. Bron's the one who knows where the Hole is.'

'*What?!* Why didn't you say?'

'I thought I did? Why would we be talking about it otherwise?'

Emily's headache kicked into overdrive. How was this man related to her?

'Pat, for the love of . . . biscuits. Tell me where the Hole is. Please.'

A long, slow shake of the head.

'I don't know. Only Bron knows. The one I heard about was at Bedlam hospital for the mad types in Southwark. Goddess knows where it is now though.'

The urge to strangle him was rising, but she needed him to explain first.

'Are you saying there's more than one? The Library's going to freak.'

'No, I'm saying there's one, and it never stays in the same place. Moves on like clockwork it does. Only Bron has the knowing of where it's going to go.' He grimaced. 'She takes a gang and they come back with wonders. But it's not enough, she says. She wants to take her magic outside, says we're being cheated.'

'But all the magic is in the Hour to keep it safe—' She stopped, her mind whirling. 'How can she know where the Hole is?'

'She says it's the eye of the fae that lets her have the knowing, but she's a liar.' He curled his lip. 'I should know, as I'm an expert in the area.'

'How am I meant to find it?'

He shrugged.

'I've no idea, and I can't help ye. Bron can't stand me. I'm only telling ye this on grounds of nieceship, and fer to cheer ye up.'

She looked at him, eyebrows raised. He shrugged.

'Well it hasn't, but thank you.' She gave him half a smile.

'Ah, what are uncles fer? Look, if I were ye, I'd leave it be. It'll sort itself out. Most things do, trust me.'

Her smile faded. 'You specifically told me not to trust you. As a cardinal rule.'

'Ahh, ye don't want to listen to a word I say. I'm very unreliable.'

'Emily?' It was Tarkus's voice echoing through the night.

'Oops, that's my cue. Stay tricksy,' said Pat.

With that, he grinned and disappeared round a corner just as Tarkus hurtled into sight from around another.

'There you are! Where have you been? Who was that man?' He stared down the street where Pat had vanished. 'I swear I've seen his face on a wanted poster.'

Emily frowned.

'No one I trust.'

CHAPTER 9

'So the Hole moves?' said Tarkus.

Emily had filled him in on everything he'd missed, although she may have forgotten to mention the whole terrier thing. Tarkus wasn't as attentive to her harrowing story as he might have been normally though. In fact, he spent most of it looking uncomfortable, shifting from foot to foot like he had an unfortunate itch in his pants.

'Yeah, I just said that. Are you listening or what?'

'What?' he said, then blinked. 'Sorry, no I am, but . . .' He lowered his voice. 'This is the heart of *Whitechapel*. The police manual says Watch officers should patrol in pairs here, at a minimum.'

Emily hadn't noticed where they were, she'd been so wrapped up in her own problems. Now she came to peer around, she had to admit that, even for Victorian London, this place was particularly grim. There was filth and refuse strewn over the street and the buildings pressed in on them. There were other shapes in the dark too, figures that could, at the most charitable, be described as 'skulking'. There was furtive movement all around them.

'Why don't we walk and talk?' she said.

'Couldn't agree more, Miss Featherhaugh,' said Probationary Inspector Poswa, and they carefully headed back towards the noise of the main road.

'Right, so the Hole moves,' said Tarkus, who was more focused now, although he did keep looking behind them. 'And only this one Pooka, Bron, who you describe as a "mardy mare", knows where?'

'Yeah. This is much more complicated than I thought it was going to be,' she sighed. 'I was mainly hoping to discover more Hula Hoops, maybe a smuggled stack of Monster Munch, and be back in time for hot chocolate.'

She chewed her lip as they walked.

'Also, I was kinda hoping that once we'd saved the world it would stay saved, y'know?'

'Well, the Library did say this was only a leak. There's time yet.' His jaw was clenched in a very determined manner. 'I'm sure the combined might of the Watch and the powers that be can track this Pooka down.'

Emily turned to him. 'How's that gone before?'

He wouldn't meet her eye. 'Admittedly your brethren are . . . somewhat elusive.'

'Mmmhmmm,' said Emily. 'I can't even ask Mum because I'm not supposed to be— WHAHH!'

She screamed and dodged with a flare of Pooka speed as something flew through the air and just missed her head.

'What the heck?' She gulped as she saw a stone arrow stuck in a door on the other side of the street, still quivering.

'What indeed?' Tarkus eyed the street around them, his hand firm on his truncheon.

'I warned you this was a rough neighbourhoo—'

He broke off, and stared fixedly behind her, his mouth wide open. A sharp smell of mustard seeds came from him and hung on the chill night air. She followed his gaze. He was looking at a high-spired church on the corner of the street, but why? Then she froze. The whole of the old church was crawling with movement from top to bottom.

The carved stone cherubs either side of the door were thrashing around and brandishing their little bows and arrows. Their eyes were wide and their mouths gnashing and mouthing silent words. The arrow was missing from the one on the right's bow too. Little git! Above them, gargoyles with spouts for mouths and horned heads writhed in place on the wall. Moss crumbled from them as they thrashed carved wings and reached out clawed hands to point straight at her. Worse, though, were the vast stained-glass windows. They were full of saints, robed kings, and cloaked women holding haloed babies, each of them impossibly moving. The windows creaked and bowed out of their frames and the grey lead shifted as all the martyrs, wise men, shepherds, virgins and infants pressed themselves against it. Every one of their glassy eyes glared at Emily, their hands pointed at her, their mouths spoke unheard words.

'Oh man,' said Emily. 'Not again.'

'What exactly do you mean, *again*?' said Tarkus, his flaming eyes wild.

'This keeps happening. There was this statue in the park, and then some moving tapestries at the market too.'

'How fraught with danger is your life,' said Tarkus, without taking his eyes off the shifting madness of the church, 'that you fail to mention this?' He sounded hysterical.

'It just happened!'

'Why are they pointing at you?' he said. 'Because they're definitely pointing at *you*.' He stepped away to one side, and he was right. They were only interested in her.

'What have you done now?' he said.

'I don't know!'

'Vortex!'

'Shut up!'

The creaking and groaning from the church was terrible, but there was another sound too, the same kind of millstone on millstone grating she'd heard in the park. *Oh dear.*

In the churchyard next to them, on the other side of a low hedge, the carved gravestones and tomb statuary were awaking from their slumber. A grey stone knight, face worn away under his helmet, jerked into motion and reached out to point at them over the hedge. Emily and Tarkus jumped back and clutched each other. Behind the knight, the monuments on the other graves started to shift and turn too. A reclined figure with its hands folded in prayer sat up sharply. A statue of a hooded angel creaked and groaned, showering lichen as it extended a pointing hand at them.

A change came across all of the moving figures, from churchyard to steeple. Instead of just pointing, they began, as one, to gesture, hands crooking and pulling towards themselves. The whole of the churchyard, from cherubs to stained-glass saviours to broken-down tomb knights, was insistently beckoning her in. The message was clear.

COME. COME.

Statues were wrenching themselves off tombs and starting to lurch towards Emily and Tarkus. The stone knight crunched into the hedge, which strained under his weight as his hand gestured insistently.

COME. COME TO US.

'T-Tarkus, what does it say in the police manual about this?' Emily whispered. Her feet were glued to the floor by horror. Tarkus stood rigidly next to her.

'Apply pedestrian locomotion,' he said.

'Eh?'

'Run!' he shouted, and yanked her arm to pull her with him as he did just that. His limbs flailed, corkscrewing around as he pelted down the street. Not elegant, but effective. Emily put her head down and did some not-elegant legging it herself. Behind them, the church and all its awakened occupants screamed silently in frustration.

Tarkus had hailed the nearest spectral horse-drawn cab, pushed Emily into it and shouted an address to the bolt-necked, square-browed driver. Now they were spinning through London's streets. She'd just about got her breath back, but still had a case of the collywobbles. What the hell was all that about? Tarkus was flicking intently through the little black police manual he'd pulled from a pocket in his cloak. He closed it with a snap and glared at her, eyes bright and manic.

'Well,' he said, 'nothing terrifying and dangerous has happened to me for ages. I had missed it.'

'Had you?'

'NO!' he snapped. 'Why didn't you tell me you were being haunted?'

'Am I?' she said. This whole day was going too fast for her.

'What do you think that was?' he asked, fingers flexing as if he was considering strangling her.

'I don't know! I've never seen anything like it.'

'Well, neither have I. Not on that scale. It was . . . I don't know what it was, apart from really not good.' He sagged back in his seat. 'The manual is clear, we need to report it immediately and seek help. That's where we're going now.'

'What? Don't be daft, we haven't got time. We need to find the Hole!'

'And how do you plan to do that while being stalked by a dangerous poltergeist *you failed to mention*?' He gave her a stern look.

'I didn't know!' she protested. 'We really need to—'

He waved the manual at her instead of replying. The gob was about to make an apocalyptic appearance but was cut off by the cab stopping and the driver pounding the roof. They bundled out and Tarkus led the way into a small Night Watch station, Emily muttering behind him. He nodded at the boggart behind the desk and disappeared down a dark corridor into the rear of the building. Emily scurried to keep up with him.

'Right, come along. Have you got any warmer clothes in

your bag? It'll be cold in there.'

'What, indoors?'

'You'll see.'

From a hidden pocket in his apparently bottomless cloak, Tarkus produced a violently yellow woolly hat and a matching pair of gloves and put them on. He looked like he was being mugged by lemons.

Emily couldn't help but smirk. 'Wow, those are . . .'

He glared at her. 'Made by my mother.'

'. . . Absolutely lovely,' she finished, innocently. He narrowed his eyes at her, then marched on. She snickered silently as his bright-yellow extremities bobbed ahead of her down the corridor. At the back of the building, they came to a thick oak door with a brass plaque on it.

INSPECTRE LEFEVRE
NON-CORPOREAL DIVISION

Emily read the sign then gave Tarkus a withering look. 'At least he's not called the "Night Inspectre", I suppose. Come on, let's get this over with.'

She reached to knock on the door, but it creaked menacingly and opened before she could touch it. There was no one standing behind it and the room ahead was completely dark. A gust of chill air rushed past them into the corridor and Emily's breath fogged before her as she shook her head.

'Right, it's going to be like that, is it?'

She took a step in, Tarkus at her side, and jumped despite herself when the door abruptly slammed behind them, leaving them standing in the dark. There was a pregnant, skin-prickling silence, and then a deep and throaty groaning came from a dark corner, followed by a rattling of chains. Emily twitched, but refused to react. A glowing green witchlight slowly illuminated the room, showing a mildewed desk and chairs. The light was coming from a stone sarcophagus in the corner, propped upright. The lid creaked open with a groan, and a cloud of fog poured out of it, ivory, grey and white, tinged green by the glow. It pooled on the floor, then, as if filling up an invisible glass, it piled up and up until it reached head height in a column that shifted into the shape of a man in a suit with tails. He had a long, angular face, and glittered in the dark. This foggy night-light floated towards them.

'Who disturbs my rest?' His words came as from an underground river, echoing and deep.

'Erm, it's me, sir. Probationary Inspector Poswa. We met on the training night?'

As he spoke, there was a clattering noise behind Emily and she jumped straight in the air. A small wind-up monkey toy jigged past her on the floor clashing a pair of cymbals together. That was quite enough.

'DO YOU MIND?' she shouted. 'I'm having a very difficult day and this isn't helping!'

With that, the witchlight brightened up a little, and the inspectre's foggy feet touched the floor.

'Ah, my apologies. Force of habit.' He smiled apologetically and dimmed his sparkles somewhat. 'What can the restless dead do for you, young Poswa?'

By the time Tarkus had explained, along with Emily providing extra details about statues and tapestries, Inspectre LeFevre was frowning. Emily, meanwhile, was increasingly envious of Tarkus's awful knitwear. It was really parky in here. The Hog was scurrying around in her pocket, and she suspected he was making a nest out of sweet papers to hibernate in.

'What you're describing does sound superficially like a haunting, but not one the phantom community would carry out,' said the inspectre. 'We've got certain rules of conduct, you know.'

'Phantom community?' said Emily, her head still spinning.

'Yes. People of non-corporeal existence. Admittedly, since we came within the Hour there are fewer Daylight victims – I mean corporeal participants – for them to haunt, so they might have been tempted, but this is beyond the pallid.'

'You're telling me! A whole church just went full horror movie on me!'

'This is exactly my point. It's most unusual. What you've experienced . . . it's incredibly difficult to animate the inanimate. Dolls and articulated toys aren't much of a challenge . . .' The monkey gave a twitch of the cymbals on the floor, and Emily flinched then glared. The inspectre didn't seem to notice. 'Tears of blood are ten a penny, but to turn a statue's head, or twist a tapestry? Let alone a whole church . . .' He shook his head, leaving a trail of glowing motes as he did. 'That's beyond even a class five full-roaming vapour. No, a worryingly powerful entity is behind this.'

He floated closer to Emily and his glowing foggy hand rested on her arm. His fingertips didn't move her sleeve, but her arm went as cold as if she'd plunged it through ice into Arctic waters.

'If it's malevolent, you are in great danger,' he said.

'I don't know what a "mullivant" is, but it *definitely* looked dangerous, I can promise you.' Emily rubbed her temples with both hands. 'Why is it haunting me though? What have I done?'

The inspectre floated back and rotated slowly in the air. He rubbed his chin in thought as he spun.

'I don't know. Any family curses? Recent purchases of terrifying dolls?'

'Not unless you count having to live with my mum, and nope.'

'Have you committed any egregious sins?'

'Like the bird?' said Emily, who wondered why that kept coming up. Tarkus groaned behind her.

'*Egregious*,' said Inspectre LeFevre. 'Particularly awful. Have you done anything bad?'

Tarkus snorted.

'Oh! Loads!' Emily stared up into space and her tongue crept out of the corner of her mouth as she tried to count on her fingers. 'Erm, I lost my temper with grumpy Grinch the physics teacher and said he looked like a giant boiled egg in a bad suit, I left hedgehog poo in my chocolate raisin box when manky Manda kept stealing my lunch, I sometimes pick my nose and wipe it on the back of the sofa . . .'

She stopped; they were both looking at her aghast.

'Ahem,' coughed LeFevre, 'are any of these people now deceased? Not the sofa.'

'What? No. Even Manda only went a funny colour,' said Emily.

'Then it's not them. And the sofa thing is a disgusting habit. Stop doing it.' He breathed out a fog of cold mist. 'Unless you have wronged a powerful force without realizing it, I really don't know.'

Tarkus looked meaningfully at her, eyebrows raised so high his helmet moved.

'Erm, I may have seriously upset the Nocturne. I kind of dropped a large bell on her.'

The inspectre flinched. 'Oh dear, you're *that* Emily? Well, that must be it. But –' he paused and rubbed his glittery chin – 'wait, have any of these manifestations been musical in nature?'

'I think one of the angels had a harp, but not really.'

'Then, thankfully, it is not her. The very essence of the Older Powers would come through, even in a non-corporeal form,' said LeFevre, fading in and out of existence as he talked. 'The level of power you are talking about is similar to hers, though, but you may thank your household demons that she is not the one.'

'Wait, does my household have demons?' said Emily.

'Oh yes, everybody's does, you see they're—'

'Thank you, Inspectre,' said Tarkus loudly and clearly. 'We must get on now. Is there anything else she can do?'

'Against an entity this powerful with what appears to be a grudge?' He was already floating backwards, hands folded across his chest. 'My darkness, no. You're totally doomed.'

'What?!' shouted Emily.

The inspectre whooshed back into the fog and drifted into his sarcophagus, which shut with a bang. There was the muffled but distinct clatter of a mop falling over and taking a bucket with it, followed by a muttered curse. His voice drifted from the tomb.

'Hauntings are driven by unfinished business. Find out

what it wants and you might have a chance.' The office plunged back into darkness. 'But as I said, you're probably doomed. Ta-ta for now.'

CHAPTER 10

They stood on the front step of the police station, overlooking the shadow-filled street, and Emily shivered. This place had been scary when she'd first crossed over; a moonlit Midnight world of monsters, many of them keen to eat her, but she'd made friends here, good ones, and realized that the Night Folk were all just people. Deeply odd people, sure, but generally just as much Folk as they were Night. Since that revelation (and with nobody trying to eat her for ages) it had started to become somewhere safe. Another home. Now, with this new threat, she had a nasty feeling that she might have been hiding from the monsters under the covers all along, and they were about to rip the duvet off. It was different here now, it was dangerous, and she was just a confused girl with a possibly magical pocket hedgehog. Before, the silver moon had been a comfort, but now it cast shadows that anything could be hiding in. For the first time in a long time here, she was afraid.

Obviously the only thing to do was to drown it in misdirected anger. It normally worked.

'Nice one. Old Floaty McFloatface was loads of help,' she snapped at Tarkus. 'All "It's super bad but I don't know what it is. Doom doom doomy doom." *Great*.'

He held up a placatory hand. 'At least it makes our next move clear. We must seek out the Library, tell her what we have learnt of the Pookas' highly illegal Hole.'

'And,' he continued before she could butt in, 'we must also seek her protection for you against whatever this awful force is.' His smell was of balsam and his face was all concern. The fact he was properly worried could not be a good sign. 'The inspectre is . . . opaque, but he's rarely wrong. Perhaps you'd be safer out in the Daylight?'

'Now just a minute,' she bridled, then stopped. 'Daylight . . . oh *so* not good.'

In a cold sweat she scrabbled in her jacket pocket. As she tugged at the end of the silver chain of her night watch, it tumbled out into her hands and what had been a muffled tinny sound became the loud liquid peal of very tiny huge bells. This was the alarm her dad had helped her set. The alarm telling her she needed to be at the Night Post and ready to go way before midnight.

A sickening horrible lurch in her stomach made her stagger. She popped the watch open, and as the clock tower sproinged out of the case, she held it up and examined it, praying a closer look might change what the time was. Nothing changed, although it did start bonging louder.

'What's wrong? You're paler than the inspectre.'

'I've totally blown my curfew. I'm supposed to be at the Night Post so I can go home with Dad at the end of his shift.' She cast around frantically. 'I've got to go!'

He glanced at the clock faces and drew in a sharp intake of breath. 'It's miles from here. You'll never make it, even in a cab. You'll have to go through a local door.'

'But my dad's waiting for me, and I'll still have to get home on the other side . . .'

'If you miss this midnight, it'll be a whole other night before you can go.'

Where had all the time gone? Where? She'd had hours and then she'd gone to investigate, and then they'd been chased and . . . all the hours were gone.

'Oh, I'm so dead,' Emily gulped. 'I've blown curfew so much I might as well emigrate. Unless . . .'

'Yes?' Tarkus leant in.

'I could fake my own death instead. Leave a pile of

clothes on the beach, stowaway to somewhere foreign and hot.' She nodded to herself. 'Get a job at a beach cabana. I'd have to get a stick-on moustache for disguise purposes.'

He poked her in the arm.

'Are you talking complete nonsense rather than going home to face the doubtless richly deserved music?'

'Maybe,' she said, staring at her shoes.

'I'm afraid you're in the wrong company to hide out from justice,' he said, and tapped his badge. 'However, I do have the Master Key, and there's a door near here.'

They walked down the street to an old black-and-white timbered pub, The Dragon's Flagon, whose sign showed a very rotund reptile cheerfully drinking from a knight's helmet.

Tarkus led them to its ancient oaken side door, dug in his coat and produced the big glowing key Emily had seen earlier. He whispered a charm under his breath.

'Moon's light, preserve the night. This door's ward, by the Accord, I bid thee open.'

The Master Key blazed brighter and pulsed with light. As Tarkus held it to the lock, the key appeared far too big, but with a shimmer and wriggle that made Emily blink, it slid straight in. Tarkus checked his own night watch for the countdown to midnight, when a door in the spell could be opened.

'Ready?' said Tarkus.

'No moustache?' she said in a tiny voice.

'Not even a whisker. Come on. It's best to get it over with, in my experience.'

Tiny bells chimed, the key turned with a satisfying clunk, and a door from midnight to midnight swung open.

On reflection, Emily thought later, it was not best to get it over with at all. Leaving it for as long as possible, maybe until the people involved had died of old age or gone batty enough not to remember it, would have been much better. Things had not gone well when she'd got back. Not well at all.

It had taken her another hour and a half after midnight to get back across London on a horrid night bus. She couldn't even phone, because she'd left hers at home so it wouldn't blow up in the Hour.

When she'd got in, the lights had been on downstairs, the only house in the street where they were, and her parents had both been sat in the kitchen drinking coffee.

'We're not angry,' her dad began as she walked in.

'*I AM!*' her mum shouted.

'We're not angry,' her dad said again, shooting her mum a look, 'but we are very disappointed.'

'Urgh,' groaned Emily. 'I knew it. Look, it wasn't my fault.'

'Oh and it never is!' said her mum.

'Maeve,' her dad said, but her mum was already stalking across the kitchen towards her (although it was more of an angry waddle, because of the baby bump). She got right up close and sniffed Emily's coat suspiciously.

'Oh, absolutely reeks of magic she does. What's been going on?'

'Look, there's a serious problem – a Hole in the Hour. The Library asked me to investigate and then there was this tapestry and then Pat legged it and—' She stopped, but it was too late.

Her mum's eyes flared with anger. There was no magic here, but they nearly turned red anyway.

'*Pat?!*'

'Maeve,' her dad said again, but her mum was far past listening. Emily couldn't talk. There was so much to explain but it all jammed up in her throat.

'And I only asked ye not to do one thing.' Her mum wasn't shouting, but using her furious whisper. Bad sign. *Really* bad sign. 'One thing, and here ye are telling me that was the thing that ye have done!'

'But I didn't—'

'No more of yer lying!' Her mum was pale with fury.

'I haven't! I didn't mean to. I didn't know it would be Pat, and then he led me to the clan, and there was a big row and then Mammy Espeth made me change, and I couldn't, and I ...'

And then Emily was crying. She had never meant to, but there it was. Her mum's face was white and grim as bone, but then she sighed, and reached over and squeezed her arm.

'Okay. It's okay. It was too soon for ye to be in there alone, that's what I was trying to tell ye.'

Emily's vision was distorted by tears.

'No! This is important. I have to help.'

'Ye need to stay safe. It's no game in there. Ye're too young for it.'

'I wasn't too young when I saved you both.' She was ashamed at the spite in her voice.

'I know, *we* know,' said her dad, who was standing with her too now. 'You were brave and brilliant, but how close was it to being a disaster? How many times?'

'But I'm doing an investigation. For the Library.'

Her mum and dad exchanged glances.

'Look, the Library. Ye have to understand. She's not human, she doesn't see things . . . She asks too much some-times.' Her mum's mouth twisted. 'Things she shouldn't. Too much for a young girl, anyways. She shouldn't have done that without asking us first.'

'But I'm a Librarian. Like you,' Emily snuffled.

'Yeah, well, that didn't always work out too well for me, ye know. I don't want the same for ye.'

Her dad leant in.

'It's simply too dangerous. I spoke up for you before, but your mum's right. We won't risk it. Not with hostile Pooka and a crisis. Not without more training, and you can't have that at the moment, so for safety's sake . . .'

Emily opened her mouth to argue, but her mum got in first.

'Ye're totally Hour-grounded, for blatant disobedience and adventuring without permission.'

'Harry Potter never got grounded for trying to save the world!'

'No, but he did get put in a cupboard under the stairs, so don't test me.'

There was nothing more to say after that. A quiet voice inside her said, *You should tell them everything. They don't know about the haunting.* But another, louder voice said, *And if you do, you'll never be allowed out of sight ever again.* The second voice was right, even if it was wrong, and so she didn't say anything, and the little burn of being a liar, even if only by omission, stayed with her for a while after.

She was packed off to bed without her traditional post-Hour hot chocolate. Having popped the Hog in his cardboard hogbox (which was more of a hog palace these days, with all the tubes and extensions), she curled up in utter misery with the Feesh, in the same place she'd wriggled with excited joy only the day before. Above her head, the black glass Abbits her mum had sculpted continued their eternal chase, hare nose after hare tail, spinning as she wept.

And that was it. She was home and grounded from the Hour.

Being Hour-grounded was different from being grounded-grounded, it turned out. She didn't have to stay home, she just had to stay out of the magic Midnight world. In fact, her parents wanted her to reconnect with the 'real' world. It was still half-term and they encouraged her to see friends and go out and do things.

The problem was her real-world social life had gone to pot. She'd never exactly been blessed with a lot of friends due to her gob, but she'd had a group of girls she'd come up through two schools with now and they all rubbed along together okay most of the time (apart from Camilla, who'd never really gotten over Emily comparing her to a 'sad seaside donkey', but there was no solving that problem). Now, although she did see a few of them here and there, after her experiences in the Midnight Hour it all felt so meaningless. They clustered and talked about what they'd done and who'd said what or who fancied who, and she was more and more on the outside of it all and just didn't care.

Without silver moonlight and sharp shadows, everything was hollow and petty and false. The world here was so washed-out in comparison. She kept closing her eyes and seeing the bright shock of the full moon and the bone-white gleam of stars, and the stark shadows they cast, and the faces and fangs of the things that lived there. She would lose herself for whole minutes at a time, and then was sniped at for daydreaming or ignoring people. *You're wrong*, she wanted to tell them. *I'm not daydreaming, I'm NIGHT-dreaming and it's so much better.*

As the days dragged by, Emily worried constantly about what was going on with the whole Hole situation. She'd cornered her dad while he was doing compost planning to ask him to talk to the Library for her, but he'd firmly shaken his head.

'I don't want you getting involved any further, Puzzle. I'm sure Tarkus has told them everything you discovered, and the Watch have got good people to sort it out.'

She couldn't believe he was being this obstinate.

'Yeah, but they're not Pooka, are they? They won't be able to find them!'

He put his flat pencil down on his bit of card. His eyes were gentle but his expression was firm.

'That's the end of it, Puzzle. It'll all be fine, I promise.'

'Argh! You're worse than that eejit Pat!'

She stormed off, kicking his compost bin on the way out. That nearly got her grounded-grounded. Never mess with a man's compost.

It was all dreadful and the fact she had to listen to Big Ben chiming from her bedroom window at night just made it worse. She was colossally grumpy, and she spent a lot of time muttering at things. She'd decided birds were much too noisy, for example, and that people whistling outside should be banned. Or executed. Her and her mum were avoiding each other like angry cats; they circled sofas and tables so as not to cross paths. It was like being back in the bad old days of pre-Midnight Hour parental strife, but this time it probably was her fault, even if her parents were being totally unreasonable. If she was honest with herself, she'd admit she pushed the investigation too far. She had known it wasn't okay, but had just . . . done it anyway. Why had she? She just wanted to . . . to do it all herself. To have an exciting life. To be, she hated to think it, more grown-up. *Hmmm.* Self-examination wasn't much fun, she decided, particularly when you were probably the problem.

She was a gruffly ball of doom sitting scrunched up on her bedroom floor. She couldn't even read, she was in that much of a grizzle. She let out her third largest sigh ever and looked at Hoggins, perched relaxing on the top sun deck of his ever-growing hog-tower.

'There's only one thing for it, Hog. It's time to run away.'

CHAPTER 11

Obviously, she wasn't actually running away. That would be ridiculous. Running Away Practice was, however, what she had taken to calling her occasional attempts at exercise. As a rule, Emily completely avoided exercise whenever possible. She was convinced it wasn't good for you, but the Midnight Hour had changed that. She'd first had the urge to try running in the real world some months after the whole saving the unreal world thing. Somewhere in there, between all those life and death chases, and the hectic headlong joy of her first sprint as a hare, a faint interest she'd never expected to experience had stirred.

She'd snuck out on a couple of nights when she was absolutely certain not to see anybody she knew, with her old battered PE trainers and a dodgy charity shop tracksuit of her mum's, and run round the block. It was difficult to find the enthusiasm when not being chased by ghastly things with sharp teeth but, nevertheless, when she drew to a halt, not that many minutes later, huffing and puffing, she'd felt a small sense of . . . she wasn't sure what. Pride? Achievement? She'd kept doing it after that.

She told herself it was mainly about being more effective at running away, but she found a certain satisfaction in the simple act of running. Transforming into a hare was one thing, but this, her feet and legs carrying her along faster and further night by night than she'd ever thought they could, was a type of magic that worked in the Daylight realm too. It was not like her, and she didn't want to look at it too closely in case she came to her senses and stopped doing it. But for now she would run, a couple of nights a week, and it was hers. This also meant she was allowed to eat a *lot* more biscuits for 'necessary fitness energy', and was doing so.

Running was also a good releaser of the terrible inner grump and she needed that right now. She donned joggers, trainers and a hoodie, then scooped the Hog out of his little box and popped him into her big pouch pocket. She jammed her phone in her joggers pocket but didn't take earphones, as she liked to listen to what was going on around her. She bounced through the kitchen doing the bendy leg walk she used to warm up.

'I'm going for a run. Back later.'

'Okay,' said her mum in the flat tone she'd been using of late, then looked at her pouch. 'Is that the Hog? It can't be good for him.'

'He likes it. It lulls him to sleep.'

'He's a hedgehog, not a jog-hog,' her mum said, but Emily was already bouncing out the door.

After the first fairly dreadful five minutes, her legs warmed up, her breathing settled, and her world shrank down to the square metre her feet were hitting and the air coming into her lungs. It left all the things she was trying not to think about – like how she might have done everything differently – outside.

She ran out of their little street in Lambeth towards the river, and across Lambeth Bridge. She deliberately didn't look right as the sight of Big Ben would only annoy her. She had a cunning route which stayed in green spaces or quieter streets until she got to the park. She passed through tree-lined squares and through narrow older roads that might easily have been in the Midnight Hour if it wasn't for the sunlight and the cars parked everywhere. The grand old stone behemoth of Westminster Abbey loomed to the right, and with a zig and a zag and a bit of a jigger, she cut through a footpath or two, and was out on the edge of St James's Park.

She crossed the road and breathed in the fresher air with relief. She fell into the loose loping jog that allowed her to take in the trees and the sky and headed straight for the lake to see the pelicans. The huge waddling birds were like magical creatures in their own right, too big and too beaky to be real. She came out higher up on The Mall, so as to avoid the tourist mayhem outside of Buckingham Palace, and made herself a deal. If she did one lap around Green Park, she was allowed to go back and get syrupy waffles from the stall near the Palace. Thus incentivized, she turned left down the avenue of trees on the Constitution Hill side of the park, admiring the gleam of the Palace's stonework over the road. Everything was feeling a lot simpler now . . . until it suddenly got a whole lot more complicated.

The oddest feeling came over her. What was it? It was familiar and wrong all at once, it was an electric prickle across her skin, a twitch in her nose, and a distinct tingle in her ears. It was the ears that gave it away. The Pooka part of her was waking up, but out here in the real world! As fast as it came it had gone again. Had she imagined it? She came to a halt, breathing hard, as much from excitement as running. She didn't know if she was listening or looking. She walked back, head tilted, nostrils flared, all her senses primed. Surely she'd imagined . . . no! There it was again. All of a sudden her whole Pookaness flared up. It wasn't at full strength, more of a tingle. She couldn't change shape, but her senses were heightened and a little roil of heat and untapped power throbbed in her chest.

She sniffed and sniffed, and her nose twitched, and she could smell traffic and pollution and really quite a lot of dog poo, but also the pelicans in the park and the sap in the trees and the moss in the nests of birds. How was this possible? The only thing that could do this to her was . . .

'Magic,' she whispered. 'There's magic here.'

How could that be? She spun slowly, arms out for balance, and tried to orient herself towards it. She had a sudden vision of how she must look and stopped spinning and instead squatted down as if she were stretching. Runners did odd stuff all the time, people would think she was de-twanging her calves or whatever. She closed her eyes and concentrated. The tingle of impossible magic was coming from the other side of the road. On her side was the avenue of trees that lined the park edge, on the other were sharp waist-height railings fencing off a wide grassy strip dotted with mature trees. Beyond this was the tall brick wall, topped with nasty razor wire, that marked the rear of Buckingham Palace and its gardens.

Her more sensitive Pooka nose homed in on the signal. The magic was somewhere the other side of the railings.

Her mind raced. Magic in this world should be totally impossible; it was all locked up in the Midnight Hour to stop it from leaking. If it was here it was because it *was* leaking. Could this be the Hole? She had to find out. She was about to cross the road to do so when she saw something even more shocking than magic in St James's.

It was Bronagh, walking up the hill towards her, on the other side of the road.

Emily's body reacted before her brain had fully processed the information. She blurred into warp speed and wedged herself in behind one of the big trees that lined the path, all pressed up against the bark and gasping. She took a breath to calm herself and ever so carefully peeked back out.

It was definitely Bron, out in the Daylight realm. She was ghost-pale and carrot-topped, and where the sun caught her those colours glowed like candle and flame. If a candle had been dressed up as a goth princess with big sunglasses, anyway. Her clothes made more sense out here. She looked London goth-punk cool, although the canvas 'I ♥ London' bag over her shoulder was off-brand. Bron glided along with the same effortless grace Emily had noticed before, utterly confident of her place in the world; any world apparently. She gave no sign of having spotted Emily, and Emily breathed a sigh of relief.

Bron walked to nearly opposite Emily's hiding place,

and with no more than a glance over her shoulder, grabbed the top of the railings and vaulted over in a move so smooth that even Emily was impressed.

'Show-off,' she muttered. Bron walked across the grass strip to the razor-topped wall. Was she going to try and climb that too, and, if so, exactly how long would it take for armed police to appear? This might even be fun. Bron ran her hand along the wall, stepped out of view behind one of the bigger trees and . . . totally failed to reappear. *Eh?* Where had she gone? Emily craned her neck to look either side, but there was no sign of her. She'd disappeared.

'Things, Hog, have just got real,' she said. 'Where's Watson when I need him, eh?'

Some might argue, she mused, that this would be a really good time to tell a grown-up. These people would be wrong. It risked losing Bron's trail and, worse, would lead to an inevitable pat on the head and all chances of adventure being taken out of her hands.

'Not asking permission, Hog, is the new asking permission.'

From the depths of her hoodie pouch, the Hog gave a disapproving grumble.

'Better to seek forgiveness than be told a flat out "no way" in the first place, I reckon. Don't you?'

The Hog's silence, she presumed, represented enthusiastic approval.

Having hazardously crossed the road, getting over the railings was, Emily found, not as easy as Bron had made it look. Firstly, she felt terribly obvious and guilty. Odd how she had done so many brave and adventurous things in the other world, but doing it here and now in daylight she felt like a child, like someone was going to tell her off at any minute. Or, more likely, arrest her for trespassing on royal property. She shook it off. She was an empowered woman with her own mission and a hedgehog, and would not waver. Although the railings *were* pretty pointy. Having checked both ways for witnesses in a totally non-suspicious manner, she hauled herself up so she had one trainer on the top of the rail, and a point in each hand, and with an undignified straining noise, launched herself over. There was an awful moment when her joggers caught on one of the spikes and it looked like she might end up trapped upside down with her trousers round her ankles, but with a ripping noise, she fell free and broke her fall with her face.

Smooth like a panther, she told herself. She levered herself to her knees, soothed the thankfully unsquashed Hog, and tried to spot where Bron had gone. She could see the other side of the tree now, and Bron wasn't there. Emily looked up into the branches in case Bron was playing some cruel 'jump on Emily's head' game, but no, she had completely vanished. In her place was a growing pulse of magic. It was much, much stronger here. Feeling very exposed to curious passers-by, she scooted over to where Bron had vanished. Her footprints were clearly outlined in the flattened grass and where they stopped at the wall there was ... *What* was *that?* She had to rock from side to side to glimpse it, but there was a thin skein of shimmering gold hanging in the air, flat against the wall. A line of gilded sparkle forming a golden hoop, six foot high and wide.

This was where Bron had disappeared. This was where the magic was coming from. She'd found the Hole.

Now she'd glimpsed it once, it was easier to spot. The sunlight was different where it passed through and the brickwork was oddly distorted behind it, like looking through a goldfish bowl. She stared at it and through it, lost in thought. This was her moment, this was the chance to follow Bron and seize adventure by the tail and crack the case and prove she should have been allowed to do it all along. She took a step forwards, then hesitated. It was also a chance to stamp on any form of trust between her and her mum and dad who, she would be forced to admit (under torture) were actually pretty okay really. She eyed up the glinting circle and gave a firm nod.

'You know, Hog. I am not a complete idiot.' There was a gurgle from her pouch that she chose to ignore at this point. 'This would be a good time to tell Mum and Dad what's going on. Check out my new-found sense of responsibility,' she sighed.

As she reached to extract her phone from her joggers, the breeze caught a strand of her sweaty hair and blew it, ever so gently, into contact with the shimmering gold that hung beside it. As her hair touched the Hole, a zap of magic passed through her that left her wobbling. Then, as if her hoodie had been caught in a train door, she was yanked first sideways then upside down by an unstoppable force. Before she'd taken another breath, she was hurtling into a tunnel of light. Anyone watching would have seen her jerk, blur and vanish. All that was left behind was the floating sound of her yell.

'OH, COME ON!'

CHAPTER 12

It isn't a hole, it's a whirlpool, she thought as she was spun and turned and topsy-tailed until there was a rising possibility she was going to be horribly sick. She was being thoroughly rinsed and tumbled and developed a lot more sympathy for the socks she chucked in the washing machine every week. There was nothing around her but golden light and a sense of enormous power frozen but creaking against its bonds. A power she was hurtling through and bonds she was loosening with every nauseating spin. She gripped tight at the pouch of her hoodie to stop the Hog being spun off into the cosmos, but there was something else in there. Something vast and heavy, bigger than the power that spun her even, but she couldn't move her head to see what it was. As she travelled, the light changed gradually from white and gold to silver and black and she hurtled into shadows and moonlight.

It lasted for an eternity, then it was over. She was spat out to find herself in the air and falling, but had no time to scream before she landed on a thick velvet sofa and bounced straight off on to a much less padded floor.

'Ow ow OW!'

Her hands were touching soft carpet. She saw them silver-tinted against the monochrome pattern, and screwed her face up. With great reluctance she looked up to see a floor-to-ceiling window, through which shone the sudden full moon, swinging huge out of the darkness and standing luminescent in the sky full of stars. Just to rub it in, the silhouette of a pointy-hatted woman riding a broom whizzed across it.

'Ohhhh man, Mum is *never* going to believe me.'

Emily hauled herself to her feet and checked the Hog, who was upside down again and very annoyed about it, but otherwise okay. She was in a long corridor with a carpet runner, high ceiling, and big windows all along one wall that showed a vast and dark courtyard. There was the suggestion of a lot more building around it by the size of the shadows that loomed over the space, but she couldn't make it out. All was eerily quiet. On the wall opposite the windows, not far from where she was standing, were a pair of gilt-encrusted double doors, gleaming in the invading moonlight. The corridor disappeared off into the distance in both directions, with the occasional sofa scattered along it for the weary, and those dropping in from another dimension. *Dropping in . . .* She looked up. The Hole was here too, and easier to see in the darkness. It hung, glinting, flat on the wall above the sofa. Here the moonlight changed its glimmer to that of burnished copper, not gold, and it was a ring of fire.

Emily gave it a wickedly cross look, and carried on figuring. Hole located – that was one major job off the list. Now she just needed to locate herself. Where was she? Not on the strip of grass on Constitution Hill, that was for sure. What she did know was where Bron had gone. There were a couple of muddy footprints on the carpet leading to the shiny double doors, but she hardly needed them. She'd been able to get a hint of Bron's scent outside with the touch of magic but now, back in the Midnight Hour, her Pooka nose meant she could pretty much *see* the trail of leather, angst and hair product Bron left behind.

Okay, crisis meeting with self time. What was she supposed to do? She needed to tell the Library where the Hole was, and figure out a way to explain this to her mum without being sent away to child prison. If she'd got a pen she could write it down and the Library would know immediately, but she'd only got her joggers on. Shame she couldn't text . . . *Oh no, the phone!* She'd brought it into the Midnight Hour, which meant it'd be exploding any moment. She fished it gingerly out of her pocket. Funny, it didn't look like it had been through a microwave. The screen was blinking and tacky to the touch but it was working (not that there was much phone signal in the nineteenth century, of course). That was good, but also really bad. It meant the Library was right. The magic level in the Hour was dropping, all down to this stupid Hole.

She gave the Hole another hard look. Should she try to get back through or follow Bron? The decision was taken out of her hands as the Hole shimmered and started to vibrate. It became totally visible, a burning copper ring which started to spin, first slowly then faster and faster. It spun fast enough to appear a golden ball, not a ring, and then, with the frictionless movement of a soap bubble blowing on the wind, the Hole drifted away. She jumped for it, but it was too late. It drifted off up the corridor in a long sweeping arc of movement that took it through the wall and out of sight.

'Brilliant. Just brilliant.'

So it *did* move. Job of Hole location – back on the list. She gave a long, weary, disgusted sigh. Today was really starting to suck. Well, according to Pat, Bron was now the only person who knew where the Hole was, or where it was going, at least. Emily had to follow her, that was clear. She listened at the keyhole of the gilded doors, but there was only more of the same quiet that filled the corridor. She leant on the handle, winced at the squeak, and pushed one door open.

'Erm, hello?'

The room beyond was eye-popping. It was high-ceilinged and cavernous, and lit with a hanging garden of frothing crystal chandeliers. The walls were decorated in red velvet and gold detailing, with the occasional vast gilded mirror. The carpet was red too, and would easily have covered a football pitch.

'Subtle,' she muttered to herself.

At one end, raised on a dais under a flowing red canopy fringed with lacy tassels, were two very impressive chairs, with golden frames and luxuriant red cushions. They were the size of thrones. In fact, they *were* thrones. In a giant glitzy room. There was a word for that, wasn't there?

'Ah,' she said, then immediately clapped her hand over her mouth as the sound echoed around the now inhospitable-feeling throne room. It was, she reflected, probably a good time to leave. Really, really quietly.

She sniffed the air. Bron's trail went straight across the room and towards the giant doors at the other end. Of course it did. She was walking quickly across the thankfully thick pile carpet when the sudden sound of marching footsteps came from outside. She didn't have a moment to peg it before the doors crashed open.

Two tall soldiers in red uniforms and giant black furry hats crashed in. They carried rifles with glowing wands sticking out underneath the barrel, and they were pointing them at her.

'Hold it right there!' one of them shouted in a shrill, squeaky voice.

She held it right there, and put her hands up.

'Whoa there. I know this looks bad, but—'

'The prisoner will not speak.'

'Or move.'

Both of the guards' voices were high-pitched and scratchy. It took her a moment, mainly because of the blinding terror, but she realized she couldn't see their faces. She couldn't see them because their giant black furry hats started right at the collar line of their red uniforms. Had they pulled them down?

'If I can just explain—'

'The prisoner will not speak!'

The guard on the left cocked his rifle and his wand started to pulse ominously. He moved in a clunky mechanical way, and was oddly rigid. The hands holding the wand-rifle were both carved from wood. The big black hat sat on top of his shoulders where his head should be, and there was a ripple of movement in the fur. Were those gleaming black eyes at the top?

'Guys, you need to calm down. I'm a Librarian and—'

'SILENCE!'

The end of a purple-sparking wand was jammed under her nose, but she barely noticed because it was the *hat* that was shouting at her. It had beady black eyes, a tiny nose, and a wide mouth, all covered in black fur. She thought it was just a big head, then realized there were thin limbs thrust down inside the collar of the soldier's uniform. It was some kind of creature sat on top of a wooden soldier, piloting it.

She was almost too curious to be scared, but the hat was giving her serious eyeball and she wasn't sure how she was going to talk her way out of this.

'Votever is going on?' came a loud, heavily accented voice from the corridor behind Emily.

'Please, sire,' came a bone-dry and mannered voice right after it. 'The ward alarm has gone off. Please let the Bearskins handle it.'

'Don't be such a fusspot, Vardour. I shall see for myself.'

The double doors to the throne room swung open and two men entered. One had a spectacular moustache and wore a night cap and a pretty fancy purple silk dressing gown; the other had the pallid skin of the aristocratic Dead, and wore a dark suit coat with tails. The latter was performing a graceful ballet by walking side-on to the dressing-gown guy, trying to both talk to him and stay between him and whatever was in the room.

'Vot is all this?' The voice was loud, but not angry. The Bearskin nearest Emily froze, but didn't move its rifle. The other guard stood to attention.

The dark-suited Dead man, Wardour, had a withered, dry face that was very unamused.

'What is the meaning of this, boy? You face the axe for thieving here.'

Emily's patience levels were already simmeringly low. This was pretty much enough.

'I'm not a boy, deadhead! I'm on a mission from the Library to save your blinking world, and your gun-happy mate here, who is *literally* talking through his hat, won't listen.' She gestured wildly around, causing the wand under her nose to tremble, but she was too angry to notice. 'Just because I happen to have fallen through a magic hole into the treasure-filled throne room, at night, on my own ...'

She trailed off. She had to admit that sounded iffy.

'I've normally got a Library card, but I'm in my joggers.'

She was done. They were totally going to shoot her.

Wardour turned to give orders to the gun-happy Bearskin guard, but the mighty moustache guy gestured both him and the angry hat back with an imperious hand. They bowed and backed out of the way.

'Madam, ve are, of course, sorry for ze interruption, but

– 140 –

I must note that you are, in fact, in my palace, so you see my difficulty . . .' He waved a hand to indicate the general etiquette issues this was forcing on him. As he spoke, she spotted what she hadn't seen at first in the bleaching light of the moon. The dressing-gown dude was a lot less pale than his Dead lackey. In fact, behind his absolutely massive tache, he was not pale at all. He bordered on the floridly pink, in fact.

'Hang on, are you human?' said Emily.

'Vy, I should certainly hope so,' he smiled.

'It was the moustache, I couldn't tell.'

There was a gasp from behind him, and Emily caught Wardour's icy glare and winced. Then the distinct low sound of chuckling cut across them. The moustache was moving as laughter came from underneath it.

'Oh, I like zis one.' He bowed, and the tassel on his velvet night cap swung from side to side. 'Madam, might I have ze pleasure of your name? I am ze prince regent, Albert.'

'Ah,' said Emily. 'I'm Emily, and I should probably apologize about the shouting and the break-in and stuff.'

'No, no, it is of no moment. It is good to see another Daylight dweller, particularly one engaged on such important business.' He smiled, and it was a good, genuine smile. 'A pleasure to meet you, Miss Emily. Zesc men would doubtless prefer you to call me "majesty", but let's go with Bertie, as ve've been introduced.'

More rumbling from Wardour.

'Emily, you have come through your magic hole from the Daylight world, ja? Tell me, how fares the queen?'

Wardour stiffened where he was standing, and his gaze fixed upon her.

Eh?

'Oh, you know, seems good. Lots of events, lots of waving. Stacks of corgis.'

'Ah, my darling always did luff her dogs. Proud Victoria, I'm so glad she is vell.'

No one could accuse Emily of being a keen history student, but she caught up eventually. Queen Victoria! Which meant . . .

'Wait, hang on, *the* Prince Albert?' she said.

He waved a casual hand. 'Bertie, please.'

'Aren't you, y'know, dead?' said Emily, before she could stop her mouth moving.

Bertie gave her a wink. 'Ahh, a necessary subterfuge. I have been quite ill, I'm afraid, and my dearest Vicky was worried zat I might, how do you say, pop off.' He gestured at the moonlit sky through the windows. 'When she signed the great treaty of covenant with ze Night Folk to found this place outside of time, well, I came with it, a few years later. Here, I do not die.'

He sighed, and gave her the saddest smile she'd ever seen.

'But, I miss her and vait every day for her to join me. It vill be when she lays down ze great weight of the crown, of course.'

Behind him, Wardour was making furtive hand-waving efforts to get her attention. She looked over, and he made rigid eye contact, and shook his head at her.

'Ah, yeah, right. I'm sure that'll be soon, Bertie, deffo.' Totally deffo, apart from her having been dead for, like, over a century. Awks.

She was trying to find a way to make an exit, but Bertie seemed keen to chat.

'So, tell me, the peace in Crimea has held, ja? I get so little news from home.'

'Yeees?' said Emily hopefully, wishing she'd listened more in history.

'Gut, gut. Foolish to think Europe had any more wars left in her, eh?'

'More wars? After 1859? Well . . .' This one she knew! There had been at least two massive— Wardour was now shaking his head, distinctly, left to right. NO.

'Ahh, no, no. Definitely not. It's all been good out there. We're big on Europe. Thumbs-up all round.' She was sweaty and horrid all over. This was up there with the most awkward conversations ever, and she'd had some amazingly awkward ones in her time (mainly about her mum). 'Look Bertie, this has been fab, but I've got a mission for the

Library and a Hole to find and stuff. I must run.'

'Ah! Ze Library! I remember her. The tall lady who fixed everything up, along with her quiet sister. Of course, you must go.'

He waved her towards the open doors of the throne room.

'But please, Miss Emily, come back and see me. It will be refreshing to talk more vith you.'

'I will, your regalship, I promise.' And with that she did an awkward curtsy bow, that turned into a running start out of the blocks, and got out of there as fast as possible. Under her breath, she muttered, 'I am having *such* a weird day.'

Behind her, Prince Albert of Saxe-Coburg and Gotha, Prince Consort of the United Kingdom of Great Britain and Ireland, Prince Regent of the Midnight Hour, Bertie to his friends, turned to Wardour.

'Vot a fascinating child. So forthright, und such a robust build. Reminds me of my darling Victoria.'

CHAPTER 13

Head spinning from the deep and ongoing weirdness of her life, Emily looked back at the phenomenal ironwork of the gates behind her. Yup, totally Buckingham Palace. So that meant the Hole came out at virtually the same place in the Midnight Hour but not quite. Like going down a slide. Not a slide she was in a hurry to go down again, mind.

Now she was let loose back inside the Midnight Hour, without a clue where to go next. Bron's scent trail just disappeared into the welter of scents produced by the busy city, but she had to find her. Bron was the only clue to the shifting location of the Hole but her Pooka nose couldn't unpick Bron's scent from the rest of the city. Wait . . . her human Pooka nose couldn't, but what about her other ones? The awful transformation at the clan meet had been one of the worst moments of her life so far, but it had also given her use of an amazing nose. A nose that could unpick smell from smell, unwinding threads and following them back in time and round corners. A nose that 'saw' better than her eyes ever had.

'Oh, man.' That was the answer. She gritted her teeth, then a grumbling stirred from the little bulge in her pouch, and she realized there was a problem. She delicately inserted a hand in and pulled the problem out. The Hog sat blinking on her palm.

'Hoggins, I'm going to have to change, and I promised I wouldn't do that to you again, but I also promised Mum I wouldn't leave home without you.'

He nibbled at his shoulder.

'So, look, I'm going to put you in the hedge here, and I promise I'll come back for you, okay?'

She went to lower him down but couldn't. He had gripped her cuff with his claws and teeth. He was hanging on.

'Hog! I don't want to leave you either, but I've got to change and you hate it.'

He narrowed his eyes at her, but wasn't letting go. She held him back up to eye level.

'Are you sure about this?'

She couldn't have sworn to it, but he might have nodded.

'Okay, great. You're totally going to sulk about this later, aren't you?'

He may have nodded again. She kissed his little nose, and he sneezed as she put him back in her pocket.

'Okay, brace yourself for the magic laundry cupboard.'

She did her best not to think about what she was about to do. Instead, she focused on how annoyingly shiny Bron's leather trousers were. As the irritation filled her, she reached back into the wardrobe of her magic self for a furrier outfit. This time, without the whole clan watching, it came easier. She pulled herself into it, like a dog-hair jumper, and went giddy as her viewpoint dropped right down to knee level, with a whistling kettle hiss of air rushing in to fill the gap. Her human self and some vast weight she couldn't believe was hers slipped into the other space, and then she was there, four-footed and furry, and still pretty damn chumbly.

She shook her thickset terrier body, lashed her stubby little tail, and then took a big snort of air. Her brain lit up with all the fascinating smells. She fought down a strong urge to roll in a particularly reeking pile of dung on the pavement, and focused on finding Bron. It was easy with her magic dog nose; the scent trail hung in the air as a knotted cord of jade and jet. Bron smelt of black fur and dank breath and a whiff of the modern world. She must have transformed once home, but now Emily could follow her anywhere.

She trotted along on Bron's trail, reeling it in like a giant ball of string. Bron had sped out of the palace and arrow-straight into St James's Park, and Emily hurtled behind her, little legs powering her along. Unlike her run earlier, now the park was a cacophony of smells and excitement. She had to strongly resist the urge that rose up in her doggy brain to go and bark at the pelicans. Instead she stuck to Bron's scent, a glowing thread only she could see. The park was different at knee height. She weaved between people's legs and tentacles, and ducked under food-carts and hedges Bron must have hurdled. She followed the trail out of the park, and back into the busier street and grand buildings of Pall Mall.

Dogs didn't look up much, and she'd been so intent on the trail that she came back to herself with a start as the thread crossed through a line of vast pillars, supporting the frontage of a particularly impressive building. She craned her doggy neck, and the words 'Her Majesty's Theatre' shone down on her in golden letters above the portico. The jade and jet thread led around the side of the theatre to the stage door. At the door, the trail changed from the scent of a hound to a girl. The smell of leather trousers returned at the same time. Emily curled her doggy lip, sneezed on her paws and, with a shudder and rattle like an old fridge, expanded back into herself.

'Bleurghh,' she said, and leant against the wall until the dizzy spell, and the urge to sniff the bums of other pedestrians, passed.

'You all right there, Hoggins?' she asked the bulge in her hoodie pouch. She was answered only by snores.

'Typical.'

She oh-so-gently pulled the stage door open and peeked around it.

There was a dark corridor beyond, and a deathly quiet. Just visible in the moonlight from the open door were walls lined with faded old posters of banshees howling opera, and scenery panels propped against them. If this was a horror movie, she would be shouting 'Do NOT go in there!' at the idiot on the screen right now. The jade and jet thread of Bron was detectable by her Pooka senses though, and continued straight ahead. She shrugged, flicked the light on her phone on, which flickered and fritzed horribly but was just about working, and began to pick her way through the clutter. She tiptoed past it all, her phone light briefly restoring colour to gaudy posters of ogre sopranos and painted backdrops of giant hedges of rose-kissed thorns. She walked through double doors into a long, thin room with an enormously high ceiling. It was jammed full with a mayhem of hanging ropes and racks of clothes, and yet more scenery. Her phone light flickered off a huge headless monster and she nearly passed out before realizing it was a tailor's dummy in a shiny outfit. A many-armed costume gown so vast it would have fit a van, let alone a troll.

There was the strangest of sensations in here. An unusual vibration that came up through the floorboards, and made her fingers tremble, and her teeth ache. It reminded her of the plane's engine throb before take-off when she'd flown on holiday. What was it?

The far wall of the tall room was all vast curtains, and as she peered through, everything snapped into place. She was backstage, in the wings, and that was the stage out there. The stage lights were on, and the wooden floor dropped off sharply to the left, into the black space of the audience seating.

She turned her phone light off and was edging closer to the gap in the curtains when there was movement ahead of her. Bron vaulted from the blackness of where the theatre seats must be. She flicked herself around in the air to land, comfortably seated, on the edge of the stage, facing out. So cool. So gittish.

Emily ducked behind the tailor's dummy. She shivered at how close she'd come to being spotted as she peeked out from behind the sequinned bum. Bron was still there, looking out into what would normally be the audience. That made two people with a Pooka nose in here now. Oh god, what if Bron could smell her? With as little noise as possible, Emily tugged at a pile of costumes and pulled a rich velvet cape over herself. From the smell, somebody might have died in it (or, she supposed, been Dead in it) and she prayed it would cover her own.

Bron sat, back straight and perfect red hair angled to catch the light. *Ugh.* She was watching something in front of the stage intently. Emily couldn't see what, because of the stage lights. She inched away from the tailor's dummy and, draped in her new cloak, crept forward into the curtained wings, behind a stack of sliding backdrop panels showing a giant clamshell and a vast seaweed plantation. The whole stage was currently rigged up to be an undersea palace. There were vast sunken statues with tridents, a narwhal with a wicked horn frolicking with a whole shoal of mermaids, and a bronze submarine with a projecting periscope. She crouched down, and tucked herself into a fold of the thick red stage curtain. When her hands touched the polished wood of the stage boards, the strange vibration buzzed through them. It had become more powerful. It was nearly audible now, a note lower than any submarine. Shaking her head to stop the hum, Emily ever so carefully leant her nosy nose around the clamshell to see what was going on.

There was movement in the darkness beyond the stage lights. A huge shape was rising up out of the dark. At first it looked like a plant, then antlers, then a crazy piece of plumbing, but as it rose into the light, and that terrible vibration grew louder and louder, it all became clear. A massive organ was being cranked up from the orchestra pit. It was no ordinary instrument; its pipes curled up and out in unfathomable shapes, a vast peacock tail of blackened metal with glowing sorcerous light flickering around the holes. It groaned like demons leaving hell as it rose.

A small hunched figure sat at the organ, wrapped in a black, hooded cloak. Bandaged hands poked out and were pressed down on the keyboard. They lifted off and the vibration stopped. It had been the organ all along, playing music that no human could hear. The hands flexed once, pulled a number of pipestops out above the keyboard, then hammered down on it and began to skitter back and forth like crazed spiders. This time the organ could be heard. As the notes powered through them, the pipes shifted and groaned. Dust and cobwebs sprayed from the gaps at the top before being scorched into nothingness by the green flames that followed. The instrument moaned and groaned and roared and sobbed, sounding as much like tortured angels as a piece of music.

Emily was gripped by the music and a riot of emotions passed through her: sorrow and heartbreak and loss and a deep, simmering rage. Her fingernails bit into her palms as the music vibrated the bones in her chest. The cloaked figure swayed forward and back and side to side, riding the music as they pummelled the keyboard and the pipes of the organ howled. As the figure thrashed, the hood of the cloak fell back, revealing long white hair, stained ivory in parts by age, pinned up with glinting metal.

Emily couldn't have said how long the performance lasted; she lost all sense of space and time as the tide of music washed over her. It was only as the notes started to fade and slow that she came back to herself and remembered she should probably breathe. As she gasped air in, the figure played one last power chord on the keyboard of the organ. As the whole space throbbed with it, the figure sagged forward, spent. The music faded away and silence crept back in, and the organist spun around on the stool to face the stage.

She might have been the oldest woman in the whole world. She was shrunken and hunched over and her face was withered and sagging. Half of it anyway. The other was covered in a porcelain mask that held a frozen beauty in its carved lines. Against the porcelain perfection opposite, the rest of her face looked even worse – haggard and sallow. Emily didn't want to imagine how bad it was underneath the mask. The black cloak was open at the front, revealing a high collared dress of deep blue velvet, and her bandaged hands projected from the long sleeves and twined against each other.

'Do you have it?' she said to Bron.

The voice was a shock after the terrible beauty of the music. Broken and fractured, somewhere between the screech of a crow and the crackle of an old record.

'I do, I do,' Bron said. She sounded different. Not as self-assured as usual. 'I . . . before I give it to ye, there are things I'd know . . .'

The figure stared at her, with an unblinking gaze, and Bron fidgeted with unease. She started to ferret inside the shopping bag she had with her.

'Everything is here, as promised. But . . .'

Ignoring Bron, the withered figure held out a bandage-wrapped hand. Bron swallowed hard, and persevered.

'I want to know, when I will be free? When I will lead my people, like ye promised?'

The figure didn't say anything, and Bron leapt to her feet in another perfect flowing move, and started treading the boards dramatically.

'It's to be out in the Daylight world I want, in my power, leaving fear and mayhem in my wake. I demand it!'

Emily shook her head. Bron had missed a career in am-dram. The stage was the best place for her.

'Know this, Pooka child.' The ancient woman rose creakily to her feet, and pointed at Bron with a trembling hand. 'I may be harrowed and reduced but civilizations have risen then burnt while I have lived. Emperors have knelt to me, and so I *will* have your respect and obedience.'

The last words throbbed out as loud as the organ notes, and Bron blanched and bowed her head.

Now that, Emily thought approvingly, *was how you did drama.*

'I'm sorry, my lady. I forgot myself. I'm just eager to be about our plan.' Bron jumped across effortlessly to the organ platform and landed, kneeling, before the tiny figure. 'I vow to bring you back to power, my lady Melpo.'

Emily's entire tummy did a sudden double barrel roll. Oh, this was bad. *Bad, bad badly bad.* Melpo. Not a good name. It was, in fact, another name for the enemy she'd thought blown to a thousand bits. The Nocturne.

That ancient thing was the Nocturne. She was back and mixed up with Bron and the Hole.

Now that was MAJOR DRAMA.

CHAPTER 14

Emily crouched behind her curtain in the fragile shelter of a giant painted clamshell, her whole body rigid with shock. That was the Nocturne down there. The most frightening woman, no, inhuman force, she'd ever met. She had a vivid memory of being clutched by the neck while a ruthless pair of sapphire-blue eyes glared into hers. She shuddered just thinking about it. But . . . the Nocturne had been tall, nearly as tall as the Library, and beautiful and willowy (when she wasn't transformed into an ogre-like rage beast). She'd been an embodiment of grace and power. This woman below her was withered and shrunken, a desiccated wreck who was probably about a million years old.

Was this her fault? Had Emily done this when she'd covered the maddened spirit of music with a nuclear amount of cursed bad luck coins? There'd been nothing left of the Nocturne but a scorch mark afterwards. The Library had said the Nocturne wasn't dead but it would take her a very long time indeed to gather herself back into a physical form. Yet here she was, and from the sound of that music, still with some of her power. How had she come back so fast? More importantly, what was she up to with Bron and the Hole?

Bron produced a small black object from her bag and, bobbing her head respectfully, she placed it into the Nocturne's bandaged hand. What on earth was it? That was answered as Bron pulled a white tangle out from her pocket, straightened it out and plugged a set of earbuds into what was now very obviously an iPod.

The utterly unexpected sight of the ancient immortal personification of music hesitantly putting earbuds in left Emily shaking her head. Electronic things shouldn't work here . . . but they did now, of course. Like her phone: still just about functioning because of the drop in the level of magic that would normally have cooked it like a micro-wave. Bron pressed play and Emily bit hard on her own knuckle in sudden dread.

The Library and the Nocturne needed to 'feed' on new human creations in order to fuel their power, and there weren't any in the Midnight Hour. Last year, Emily had sent the Library her whole book collection to bring her back from the brink, and the Nocturne had been smuggling in old vinyl records to charge herself up during her last evil plan. How many albums were on even one iPod? This could be bad.

The Nocturne arched her back and snarled as the music began playing, a tinny, scratchy noise in the vast dark theatre. It started normally, then became faster and faster and faster until it was an indecipherable high-pitched squeal. The Nocturne's eyes glowed icy blue as it did, until the iPod buckled in her hand and flaked away into ashes. When Emily had watched her 'eat' a record before, it had filled her with a rippling power and she'd visibly become younger and stronger. Now there was still a nimbus of light around her, but the Nocturne was little changed. She stood straighter, and her eyes glowed with a little of that old sapphire blaze, but her hair stayed white and yellow as bones, and her face like worn leather. The Nocturne let the handful of ashes crumble between her fingers.

'More! I need more! I need to feast and you bring me scraps!' she snarled. 'I am vast and unchartable. I contain legions!' She sagged. 'Or I did. Now I am empty, because of that foul, idiot child.'

Oi! thought Emily.

'I must regain myself. I must,' the Nocturne said in a

quiet voice Emily could barely hear, and sat back at the organ stool, her head hung low.

Bron knelt before her, and hesitantly took her bandaged hand.

'My lady Melpo, ye've been wronged by a traitor to my clan. I will put it right.' She stared up at the immobile masked figure. 'When ye first whispered to me on the wind, I knew that I, that *we*, were meant for greater things than this prison.' Her eyes blazed with zeal now. 'Don't lose hope. Ye grow stronger every day with every gift I bring. It's just yer previous majesty that makes it difficult to see it.'

Blurk, thought Emily, *what a creep*.

The bandaged hand clutched back.

'We're so close. The Hole will open only three more times,' said Bron. 'Ye'll be strong by then, and on the twelfth, ye can set us free.'

That didn't sound good.

The Nocturne brought her other hand to clasp Bron's.

'Thank you, Bronagh. You are wise and loyal and brave, and I am lucky to have you.' She nodded and the porcelain of the mask glinted. 'You're right, we are so close. When I am free, you will be raised high at my side as the sword of darkness, and havoc will follow in your wake.'

She reached out to stroke Bron's cheek.

'I will chart the next positions for you. You must go out and bring me more of these music boxes before the final opening.' Half her face split into a nasty grin, while the porcelain mask remained unmoved. 'I *must* be strong enough for that glorious twelfth, when we shall be released.'

Emily's brain whirred. This was pretty awful, obvs, and she was trying not to think about just how scary she found the Nocturne, even without her full power. She hadn't sounded pleased with the whole being blown-up thing at all. Bron was a nasty bit of work too *but* . . . if Emily heard where the next Hole-stops were, she could fix everything. This was the chance. Her chance. She knew she'd be good at detectiving all along. She bit her lip at a sudden thought of Tarkus. She had to do it. She would do it.

Emily pulled her cloak of many odours tight around her as Bron helped the Nocturne on to the stage, oh so close to her. She tried not to breathe. How did the Nocturne know where the Hole was going to happen? Was she responsible?

The Nocturne produced a thick parchment from her sleeve and unrolled it. From the outline of the Thames, it was obviously a big map of London. Emily squinted trying to see more, but the Nocturne turned away. She nearly bit through the clamshell scenery with frustration. She didn't dare move, though. The Nocturne limped to a big treasure chest prop, and flattened out the map on top. From her other sleeve, she produced one of those two-leg pointy things for drawing circles and carefully walked it around the map.

'Now child, if the last Hole was near the centre of the palace, as I'd predicted –' she glanced up at Bron, who nodded – 'then, with the talisman of fortune at the centre of the works, its next stop will be . . .'

The Nocturne was talking under her breath, while Bron waited eagerly. But not as eagerly as Emily.

'It will be near St James's Palace, a street away at Park Place.'

Emily fizzed and had to stop herself squeaking with excitement. An actual clue.

Bron dipped her head in acknowledgement.

'Easier than Buck House, my lady.' She grinned. 'Although anything's easier than having to swim out to the middle of the Thames by Vauxhall.'

The Nocturne favoured her with an affectionate smile. Well, half of one anyway.

'Brave Bronagh. Now, be warned. We near the end of my symphony and the tempo grows faster. As the Working weakens, so the Hole moves faster around its orbit.' The Nocturne's eyes sparkled in the gloom. 'It won't stay in one place for long now. I think it best if you know where the final two locations will also be.'

Emily nodded along with Bron. This was it. Everything she needed. She was Sherlock Holmes and Batman and Inspector Gadget all in one. *Man, big extendable robot arms would be brilli—* She needed to focus. Emily was staring hard at the Nocturne, who was working more things out on the map, when she spotted something utterly terrible.

She had to blink a couple of times to convince herself it was happening. The big painted scenery backdrop at the far side of the stage, the one covered with black-eyed, sharp-teethed, frolicking mermaids in uncomfortable-looking clamshell bras; something was different about it, about them. Their long red hair had started to billow in the unseen tide. They were gently bobbing up and down, webbed fingers trailing through the seaweed, iridescent tails slowly lashing in the current. It was hypnotic. It was . . . potentially incredibly bad.

As a small mercy, Bron was gazing adoringly at the Nocturne, and the Older Power was bent over the map. This was just as well, as the movement quickly spread across the rest of the stage set. In the undersea palace, bubbles bubbled and fish lashed their tails. The periscope of the bronze submarine swivelled towards her, the narwhal aimed directly at Emily's hiding place with its horn, and the mermaids were clustering into a huddle, all pointing over at her, black eyes beady and mad.

Doom doom doomy doom doom had caught up with her. The haunting was here.

The ripple of movement was spreading into all the scenery. She was surrounded by painted boards and they were starting to writhe with that terrible animating force. She had never wanted to run so much in her life, but didn't dare move for fear Bron and the Nocturne would hear her, and she just *couldn't* before she'd heard their plan. But what would happen when the haunting reached her?

The giant painted Neptune statue hefted his gilded trident to point at Emily in the wings, the fabric of the boards bowing with a creak as it did. Bron's head jerked up at the noise.

'What in Danu's name?'

Bron was staring at the moving figures with wide eyes, but it could only be so long before she looked to see where they were pointing. Now the scenery was shaking, and forms were pressing out of the backdrops like they'd been trapped inside. Faces and eyes pleading for attention. The Nocturne hissed.

'Can it be? Is that . . .' She spun around, half of her devastated face awash with . . . not confusion. Was that recognition? '*You*. It's you!'

Emily's heart convulsed. She'd been seen! But then the Nocturne snarled and limped towards the moving scenery on the other side of the stage instead. *Eh?*

The wall of seaweed on the board right by Emily writhed as the mermaids from the other side of the stage started to appear in it. They'd swum over! She fell on to her hands and knees, desperate to get away but too scared to move. The Hog started doing a full-scale acrobatics routine in her pouch, clearly sensing imminent doom. The mermaid's black eyes glinted as they gnashed their sharp needle teeth but, now they were closer, she could see that they were not pointing at her but way over her shoulder instead. They looked more worried than angry too. She remembered what the inspectre had said: *find out what it wants, and you might have a chance.* Although she couldn't believe she was doing it, she knelt closer to the boards and whispered, 'What?'

Sure of her attention, the whole shoal of them gestured as one, thrashing their tails as they pointed behind her. They were all mouthing something too, one word, again and again. Their lips compressing together and popping out as they spoke. Emily could almost make out what they were saying. She formed the same mouth shape herself, fascinated despite the danger.

'What are you saying? Muh something? Buh something?' She set her lips to match those of the now-frantically pointing and mouthing mermaids. 'Mare? Buh air? Bare?'

Oh man.

'BEAR!'

CHAPTER 15

It was only the warning that saved Emily. She whirled around to follow the pointing fingers and an electric thrill of horror shot through her. Right behind her, incredibly quiet-footed for one so large, was her old and terrible enemy, the Bear. He loomed seven foot tall in his half-bear, half-human form, and his arms were poised to strike. Their eyes met and he lunged for her with his awful claws.

The blaze of Pooka magic in her chest filled her with speed, and she dodged his vicious swipe by barely an inch. The claws shredded her stinky cloak into tatters instead of her, then stuck in the velvet curtains. The Bear overbalanced and crashed into the scenery and curtains, with a crack of wood and a rip of tearing cloth. The mermaid-filled boards fell flat with a crash, with the Bear all tangled in fabric on top of them. It left Emily, crouched and panting, exposed for all to see.

Bron gasped but Emily's eyes were on the Nocturne. The porcelain half-face mask gleamed like a skull revealed beneath the skin. The two pinpricks of glowing blue light that were her eyes focused on Emily. A withered hand came up in a grabbing gesture, and the visible half of her mouth gaped wide.

'It's *her*. Ursus, *kill her!*' the Nocturne screamed, and though her voice lacked its old power it was still enough to crack the glass on every single lamp in the theatre.

The Bear was already rolling to his feet. Emily exploded into motion like a sprinter out of the blocks and hurled herself back towards the stage door. Behind her came a voice, an earthquake with a sore throat, one she'd never hoped to hear again. The Bear.

'MINE!'

Bad bad bad. Very bad.

She was actually, honest to god, exiting stage left, pursued by a bear. It was less fun than she would have imagined.

She sprinted through the shrouded darkness of the backstage corridor, bashing into unseen costumes and boards, but staggering on. All the posters of the past shows writhed with life now, and banshee sopranos pressed themselves against the frames, pointing back behind her, and mouthing the words. Bear. Bear. BEAR.

'Yes, *I know*. Thank you!'

From behind came terrible heavy footsteps and roars of fury as the Bear gave chase. He was a great big growling furry freight train of doom coming down a tunnel. She had no room for thought because of the fear that filled her all the way to the top. Slamming full-on into the closed door to the street brought her back to herself with a painful jolt. She clawed it open, staggered outside and kicked the door shut behind her.

The moonlight outside was bright as daylight after the dark theatre. She threw herself down the street, ricocheting off the few Night Folk on the pavement. She'd barely got halfway along the street before the Bear crashed straight through the door, boards and brick surrounds exploding out everywhere. As screams and curses came from the folk around her, she couldn't help but stop and look back at the Bear as he ripped the remains of the frame off his huge shoulders. He was as vast as ever, but had a great big pink scar down his face and neck. Was that from his fall at Big Ben? Why was she looking when she should be running?

'No escape this time, girl!'

Again, there were the most terrible stomping thuds as

the Bear accelerated to full speed, crashing down the street after her. She squealed despite herself then put her head down and ran like she'd never run before. Ran through the moonlit streets of Midnight London, with the Bear slavering at her heels. This was the nightmare she'd been having ever since she'd first encountered the Bear. Awful visions of running through dark narrow alleys pursued by a ton of snarling fur and teeth, and now she was living it. How had her life ended up with her being chased by the Bear again? How?

She'd take a haunting any day of the week. And what had been going on there? The ghost had been like, super helpful and pointy. Good at charades too, probably. Her mind, as always, was trying to think about weird things when really stressful stuff was happening, but skidding and nearly falling on the cobbles helped her concentration enormously.

She had no idea where she was, but just kept running. She'd started on the main streets outside the theatre, but now she ran pell-mell down deserted alleys and narrow-ways and snickles, navigating by instinct. Maybe she could lose him in the tangle of the lanes? She risked a glance back and he was still there, closer than she thought. Big pink tongue lolling back and forth out of his obscenely grinning fang-filled mouth, drool flying out in silver streaks as he drove his big legs down like pistons. She used a lamp post to help her corner and shot off down a side alley. His brakes weren't as good and he cursed as he missed the turn.

She'd gained a few seconds' lead, but what to do with it? Could she change and outrun him as a hare? She was definitely frightened enough.

'Sorry Hog, better inside cosmic laundry space than inside a bear, yeah?'

She reached within and groped for her hare shape, but couldn't grip it. After changing earlier she just didn't have enough energy left. She sobbed with frustration and tried again, but it was useless. Maybe if she had time to sit down and rest and concentrate, but doing it half blind with terror and exhaustion was impossible. She could hear him getting closer again but . . . she could feel another part of her magic there, one she hadn't found before.

She reached away from her other shapes, and found something loose as lightning and slippery to grasp. She knew, without knowing how, that it was her luck, or her grip on luck anyway. It was coiled and pulsing, half shadow, half light, bad luck and good. The oddest thing, but hers. What had Pat said? That she could push it? She found the shadowed side of it and, without knowing how she was doing it, pushed it back towards the Bear. As she did, she sensed his brute luck coiled around him.

Without having to think, as she pushed her shadow on

to him, she took his light. It was mercurial and squiggly and filled her chest with the warmth of Pooka magic. She had pushed her luck. Pushed the bad on to someone else and taken the good, like Pat had said. She was giddy and guilty, and sick. She risked a glance over her shoulder, but she was still being followed by about two thirds of a ton of deeply terrifying were-bear. Then, all of sudden, he stumbled on a loose cobble, and crashed over to the side of the alley. Hope leapt up in her, but he bounced off the wall and kept on roaring after her. He had barely slowed down.

'I feel your magic.' The voice was a steady running chainsaw. He wasn't even out of breath. 'You not strong enough to stop Bear.'

She'd failed. She failed at everything to do with being a Pooka. She whimpered and kept running but, with hope gone, her legs were failing. What would those claws do to her when they did?

'I'm so sorry, Hoggins,' she said.

There was a loud metallic squeak from behind her, then a deep clonging bong, like the ringing of a huge bell. She risked another glance back, then slammed the brakes on. The alley between two warehouses she'd just run through had been empty, but now a wide metal door had been swung open, blocking the alley completely. The massive door was still shivering, and showing through the thick metal was a slight bear-shaped outline, pressed out from it like a jelly mould. From behind it came a deep and anguished groaning.

Emily winced, sympathetic despite herself.

'That's gotta hurt.'

From inside the warehouse, a pretty, freckle-faced gorgon with a head covered in hissing red snakes in place of hair whistled as she pushed a trolley of hot loaves out to cool. She was wearing an apron and covered in flour, and Emily's tummy rumbled at the smell of warm bread.

'Evenin' love.' She waved at Emily and the snakes all swayed and smiled too.

Unable to speak, Emily waved back as the gorgon baker sashayed back inside with a grin. Emily jogged off round the corner, unable to believe her luck.

In her experience of running, Emily had found that sometimes you could keep going and going but when you stopped, your body realized the horrible trick you'd been playing on it and taught you a lesson by refusing to start again. Now, though the Bear was still behind her somewhere, the exhaustion of sprinting for street after street ambushed her; her calves screamed and her breath jammed in her throat. She mumbled to herself and petted the Hog gently through her hoodie as she limped her way along the street. She needed to figure out where she was, then she needed to tell the Library and Tarkus what was going on, and a good sit down wouldn't go amiss either. These productive thoughts came to an end as she rounded a corner into a courtyard and found the Bear no more than a claw's length away.

'Hello, meat snack,' he said in his avalanche of a voice.

She screamed and turned to flee, but her battered legs betrayed her and she stumbled and fell on to the cobbles. The Bear limped over to her, battered all to hell. His nose and face were all bashed up, worse now than before, and one of his arms hung limply at his side. But he was towering over her with a triumphant and very sharp grin, and there was nowhere to go.

'Have waited for this. You and flower boy hurt Bear.' Despite her horror, Emily flinched. The image of Tarkus and the Bear both falling into the darkness of the stairwell at Big Ben swam before her eyes. The Bear rubbed his swollen nose, and winced. 'Hurt Bear again. Now Bear's turn.'

His shape began to change. His damaged nose pushed all the way out into a snout, and his thick beard grew and crawled over the rest of his face and neck, like black spiders swarming. His bulk filled out and out, ballooning until the weight carried him forward on to his hands, that were now paws. The tatty tweed suit he wore gave way to the fur that covered him, and with a wriggle and a stretch, the man-bear became fully bear. His awful mouth opened wide to show all his many teeth.

'I'm guessing a written apology isn't going to cut it?' she said to him. 'Chocs and flowers?'

The answering roar was so loud, and coated her with so much drool, that she simply closed her eyes and waited for it to be over. She was just sorry she wasn't going to get to explain herself to her mum.

But then a howl split the night. A howl that went from low to high and rattled bones on the way, enough to put fear in anyone who heard it.

Emily opened her eyes just as a vast glowing white shape cannoned out of the dark and hurled itself on to the Bear. With an almighty thud of impact, he was knocked away from Emily. The two forms, the brown bulk of the Bear, and the white mass of the huge newcomer, landed in a pile on the other side of the street, and the most terrible noises began. There was ripping and growling and howling and snarling as the white blur tore at the Bear. It tossed him around as he would a normal man. They spun and whirled and snarled and there was an awful noise, a bottle-smashing-screech of a noise. It was only after it had continued for a while that Emily realized it was the Bear shrieking in pain.

The ball of light and shade rolled all the way over to the other side of the alley and smashed into the wall. With a final snarl and a shriek, it broke apart, and Emily could finally see what was going on. On one side was the Bear, still on his back, vast paws clutching at his terribly savaged nose. Blood gouted from between his paws and from long scrapes on his flank. He was whimpering, a noise Emily had never expected to hear come from him. Standing in between Emily and the Bear was a huge white wolf, smaller than the Bear but not by much. Its head and snarling mouth full of sharp teeth were all spattered with blood.

It was looking at the Bear, head low, shifting its weight from paw to paw, readying itself to spring again at the slightest sign of attack. Its subsonic growling was worse than any noise Emily had ever heard the Bear make. It set off every alarm bell in the most primitive part of her mind and gave her the urge to sprint for a cave or climb the nearest tree. It was awful, and yet . . . it didn't scare her. Her other senses, the ones she couldn't quite define, saw it as safe. What the hell was safe about a terrifying wolf-dog as big as a sofa though?

The Bear struggled to his feet and the white wolf surged forward, snarling, but the Bear had no fight left in him. His roars were now whimpers, and he scrabbled and stumbled away from the terrible beast and cut and ran, bumping into walls as he did, leaving a trail of blood behind him.

The wolf-dog howled again as the Bear fled, a blood-curdling sound of triumph. It only had one glowing red eye. The other was a black pit marked by a jagged silver scar. She'd never seen the beast in the flesh before, but as the moon shone down on them, its hulking shadow was very familiar.

The wolf rounded on her and, without breaking stride, turned into a small, white-haired, one-eyed, old Irish lady in a massive black fur coat. Mammy Espeth walked over to her, pausing only to spit out what looked worryingly like a mouthful of blood and fur on to the cobbles.

She wiped her mouth and frowned down at Emily where she sat, nerves a-jangle, in the gutter.

'S'pose it's time we had us a talk, eh?'

CHAPTER 16

'Whoa! That was incredible! And *really* horrible. You totally saved me though.'

Mammy Espeth scowled and waved the compliment away with the swipe of a grimy hand.

'Tchh, I was passing.'

Emily narrowed her eyes.

'Oh, you never were. You followed me to make sure I was okay.'

Mammy's scowl grew more thunderous.

''Twas Bronagh I followed, but in ye blundered, determined to be eaten, so now I've lost her.' She tutted, her lips pursed with annoyance.

'But I'm not bear food,' said Emily.

A shrug from the big fur coat eloquently suggested that it might have been easier if she were.

Emily struggled to her feet. She was feeling horribly wonky. Mammy stood there, not saying anything. Emily suspected it might be a tactic so other people would say something stupid first, but still couldn't help herself.

'Well, either way, thanks Nan.'

'Whut?' Mammy spluttered.

'That's what you are, right? You're my nan.'

'My name is *Mammy Espeth*. No one's calling me Nan, let alone some—'

'Some *what*?' Woozy or not, Emily was always down for an argument.

Mammy sighed. 'Aaah, this isn't getting any easier with time.'

She scooped a blackened old pipe out of a pocket in her big fur coat, stuffed it with tobacco that looked and smelt like horse manure, and then lit it with a flame that flickered briefly from the end of her finger. She puffed away, producing foul-smelling clouds of smoke, then dangled the tobacco pouch over to Emily.

'Help yerself.'

'No, thank you, I appear to have totally forgotten my hideous clay pipe.'

Emily faltered and had to lean on the wall. She wobbled

and nearly crumpled but a sudden iron-hard grip on her arm held her up.

'Steady, girl.' Mammy had crossed the space between them as fast as blinking.

'Sorry, I feel awful all of a sudden.'

The old lady tilted her head and looked closely at Emily with her remaining eye. Up close she was even more intimidating. Her gaze was as steely as her grip, and the Pooka eye glowed a deep crimson. Her pipe reeked too.

'It's because ye've pushed yer luck. Knocks ye bandy the first time. Ye need to get summat inside yer.'

Mammy rooted around in another one of her apparently bottomless pockets and produced a folded-up package of waxed paper tied with string. Emily took it dubiously and fiddled the string open to reveal a thick slab of fruit cake. She was inhaling it before she'd thought to say thank you.

'Fnkooo,' she managed, around a mouthful of moist, rich cake. 'Thithis reelygud.'

Mammy nodded, a tiny movement. Back to the silent treatment. The cake had an immediate de-wonking effect and Emily's legs steadied.

'Strong moves on the pocket cake, Na— Mammy.' She rapidly corrected herself as the eye flared red. 'Never be knowingly under-snacked, eh.'

Mammy almost smiled. 'Heh. Fairly said.'

'It's what Mum says.'

The almost-smile disappeared like it had never been.

'Pah. *Her.*'

Emily was about to give it full gob, but gave Mammy a taste of her own medicine instead. She just nodded silently and stared.

'Whut?' snapped Mammy.

'She does exactly the same thing.'

'*Whut?*' The eye was glowing.

'She only ever refers to you as "her" or "she", or sometimes "herself".'

'Ha!' The old lady cracked a smile. 'Course she does. The stubborn baggage.'

'Calls you that too,' Emily said.

Mammy's smile was a grin now. She took a long pull on the pipe and looked Emily up and down.

'God, ye look like her. Got the gob like her too. Shame about yer stupid accent, mind.'

'Look, what is your problem with my mum? Why aren't you speaking? Is it the Library thing?'

The smile vanished again to wherever Mammy kept it.

'Yer ma is dying.'

'What!'

A hand raised to settle her.

'Not right now. But quicker than any of us has the right to.'

'Oh god, I've got to go home.' Emily twitched, looking around to see if there might be a convenient trans-dimensional bus to hand.

'Aye, I doubt she has more than fifty years left.'

'What? But that's –' some rapid mental math – 'that's a totally normal time to live to!' Emily said, outraged.

Mammy shook her head.

'Not fer us. We don't die. Well, not for ages anyway, not with magic. But yer ma. Stupid, headstrong disgrace . . .' Her face filled with an infinite sadness. 'Got *involved*, joined a *cause*, and then sacrificed herself. That's not what we do. We're—'

'Beasts of ill-omen. Yeah yeah, I've heard it all off Pat before. What do you mean, sacrificed herself? She's fine.'

'Fine? *Fine?* A hundred years she'd aged when I saw her. Grey in her hair.' Mammy squinted. 'And a lot of other colours too . . . right gave me a turn.'

'Wait, when did you see her?'

'Well, I—'

'Have you been watching us?'

The lips pursed so much they practically disappeared.

'Well, whut do you expect? She's my youngest. *Was* my youngest.' Her eyes glistened as they filled with nearly-tears. 'She's not one of us anymore. She can't be, without magic. She'll wither and die with the rest of ye before a century is out.'

Emily rubbed her head, trying to understand. Mammy was waving her pipe around in agitation as she spoke, causing red-hot embers of the horse-muck tobacco to float down and occasionally spark on her fur coat.

'I tried to get her to stay inside. At least there's magic here, but, oh no, she'd got a mission and she had to hide the cussed coins and she'd fallen for a damn mortal. No offence.'

'Oh, offence definitely taken. But what has she actually done wrong?'

'SHE LEFT US!'

The shout took Emily by surprise.

'Left the clan. Left me. My little girl.' The tears weren't nearly-tears anymore, and the old lady scrubbed them off her face with the sleeve of the fur coat as if they burnt her. 'Left us for Older Powers and outsiders. It couldn't stand.'

'Wow. Have you guys ever got a mess going on here.' Emily massaged her temples with her fingers as she thought. 'If I've got this straight, let me ask one question, okay?'

The old lady gave a terse nod.

'Are you saying that when you found out you might lose her, you decided not to see her at all? Because that's, well, kinda messed up.'

Mammy's face was pale. She opened her mouth but didn't speak. Emily continued.

'She's really sad sometimes, and I think you are too. I know you're both ridiculous, stubborn, crazy, bats-in-the-attic-bonkers people but . . . couldn't you talk about it?'

'But she—'

Before Mammy got any further, Emily held up the shush finger.

'She's got a name.'

'But sh— But Maeve said she'd never have anything to do with us again.'

'Is this before or after you banished her?'

There was a mumble from inside Mammy's big collar that sounded a lot like 'after'.

'Mmmhmmm. Look, I'm occasionally a bit of an angry person too.' There was a distinct sound from her pocket that might have been a hedgehog sniggering, but she didn't let it distract her. 'And, honestly? Sometimes, when I'm angry, I don't always mean every word I say.'

There was silence from the old lady, but it was a thoughtful silence.

'I'll leave that one with you. Have you got a pen in the dead animal Tardis coat? I can write down our address and then if you want to—'

'I know where you live,' said Mammy, not making eye contact. A ghost of a pink flush brightened her cheeks.

'Mmmhhhmm,' said Emily again. 'Right, well drop her a note to start, maybe.'

'I don't hold with all that readin' and writin'.'

'*Fine.* Just come and visit. I'm inviting you.' Emily sighed, as everything else fell back in on her. 'If the Midnight world hasn't ended by then anyway.'

Mammy's gaze was flinty and sharp.

'How's that?'

'Look, the Hole is a big problem. Bron and the Nocturne are—'

'Blasted Older Powers. They're poison.' Mammy spat tobacco on to the kerb, interrupting her.

'That's not fair. The Library is a good person! She's my friend.'

'She's no person! She's a force, a *Power*. They all are, and they use people to get what they want.'

'But she saved everybody! This whole world.'

'Because it suited her.' Mammy's scowl caused deep rift valleys in her lined face. 'An' now it don't suit another one of them, and we all have to pay. Poor Bronagh.'

'Eh? Bron? She's one of the bad guys! You should have seen her creeping.'

Mammy shook her head. 'Bron's tricksy, like her ma, may she rest, but not like this.' She ground her teeth. 'Ever since she went through that first Hole outside Somerset House she's been different. I should have known someone was whispering in her ear.'

The Nocturne was lethally, magically persuasive. Emily

had nearly fallen for it herself once.

'It's probably not all her fault,' Emily said. *Whoa, learning moment. Who'd have thought it?* 'Can you put a stop to whatever she's planning now you know?'

'Ah, she's acting the rough sort, sure, but what's she done wrong?'

'She's going to unleash havoc on the world!'

'That's practically a job description for a Pooka. How'm I to take that to the clan? Particularly if it comes from ye.'

'But—'

'Ye're blood, but not thick enough for to become clan. Not without making yer bones, showing yer true Pookaness. Give me that, and I'll bring you in. Without it . . .' She shrugged.

'What, so I have to be a big scary dog? You know I can't. I'm a mutt.'

'It's not about scary. It's about being Pooka. Cleverness, front, all wild and tricksy.'

'My main hobbies are eating biscuits and reading books.'

The old lady sighed.

'And yer ma spent a lot of time scribbling drawings of horses on to every bit of spare parchment. It didn't stop her being brilliant.'

She held Emily's arm again, not with steel this time, but with a surprising gentleness and warmth.

'Look, ye've got what it takes, I can feel it. Ye saved the

world or something, didn't ye?'

'Apparently.'

'Well then, you'll find it when you need it, I reckon.'

'If you tell me the answer was inside me all along, I will throw that cake back up,' said Emily. She pressed the heels of her palm to her forehead, to compress the confusion in her brain. 'Oh god, this is such a mess. I need to find where the Hole's going, how to close it, and stop Bron and the blinking Nocturne.' She flicked her fingers up to count the things on her to-do list. 'And that doesn't even include this crazy ghost who's haunting me. Urgh.'

'It's not a ghost.' Mammy said in a quiet voice.

'What?'

'I saw it from the back of the theatre. It's not a ghost. It's a manny-fest-ation.' She pronounced it carefully. 'Not the same thing at all.'

'What's that then?'

'I thought you were the head-ucated one with all yer readin' and writin'? It's obvious, isn't it?'

'Guh?' said Emily, her keen deductive mind in full working order. The old lady gave a long-suffering sigh.

'What's it appeared to ye as?'

'Erm . . . statues, tapestries, stained glass, posters and scenery. All sorts. That's no help.'

'All sorts of what? What did I say is poison?' Mammy looked away as she spoke.

'Powers? Older Powers. All sorts of . . . they're all . . . Oh god, they're all types of art, aren't they?' The ice-cold shock of realization made her shiver. 'That's why the Nocturne recognized it. It's the last of the sisters, isn't it? It's *Art*. Art is haunting me!'

The old lady puffed her pipe and scowled.

'Blasted Powers.'

CHAPTER 17

Emily hustled across Midnight London, letting her Pooka sense guide her through the crowded streets, but barely noticed where she was going. Her head was full of Art and Music and Language, and old wars that had happened long before she was born. Full of Holes, and Great Workings, and a moonlit Midnight Hour held in a fragile, failing grip. Full of family and feuds and love that had gotten lost along the way.

There had been more talk with Mammy, promises of help and ways to find a hidden clan (apparently the back room of the Coach and Horses was a safe bet) but the important part wasn't the words, it was when two bony hands had held her cheeks, and thin whiskery lips had planted a fierce kiss on her forehead, before disappearing into the night. The kiss burnt there still and she raised her finger to touch the spot again and again as she weaved through the moonlit streets. For all the other things that were wrong or broken right now, the kiss felt right, and she would hold on to that in this ever-present darkness.

She was lucky to catch Tarkus coming out of his station. More than just *her* luck, too. It used up the last of that wriggling mercury light she had stolen from the Bear. She had a garbled, hand-wavy conversation with Tarkus; jumping up and down in front of him, and doing ghost and Bear charades as she explained. He commandeered an express pursuit carpet from the flying squad, and they were now hurtling through the sky towards the British Museum and the Library herself to tell all.

Despite the change from their usual hackney, the pilot was still a hulking chap with a large scarred forehead and bolts through his neck. *That family must have the transport job stitched up*, Emily thought. The carpet didn't fly high like she had on the post bike last year but skimmed the street at roof height. Tarkus had his eyes closed and his fingers were white-knuckled on the tatty edges of the rug. Emily was glad there weren't any phone wires in 1859, or they'd have been sliced like cheese. Tarkus opened his eyes long enough to give her a baleful look.

'I take it back, you're not a bad-luck vortex.'

'Oh, ta.'

He fixed her with his blazing yellow eyes.

'You're a lightning rod for malignant fate and chaos, and I'm the one holding the cable.'

'Oh come on! Where's the moral support? I'm having a proper naff day.'

She watched the moon blinking in and out of view as the carpet swerved alarmingly around the occassional taller buildings.

'Also, my mum either thinks I've been kidnapped, or have run off to get into here.' She shuddered. 'I reckon I've got until midnight to fix all this before my folks come in to send me to military school.'

'Amusing as I find your imminent domestic sanctions, I think there are more important things to worry about.' Tarkus gnawed at his lip. 'Hopefully the Library will know what to do.'

'Yeah,' muttered Emily, 'maybe.' She stared down at the chimney pots whipping past below.

He looked at her more carefully.

'What's the matter? You've managed once again to stumble unwittingly into trouble and wander out unscathed with useful information.'

'It's just . . . this whole haunting thing isn't what it looks like.' She knotted her fingers together as she spoke.

'I'll say. It's the insane and highly dangerous reincarnation of a missing demigod.'

'No, that's not it. She saved me from the Bear.'

'So you think.'

'She did!' Emily thumped the carpet, which wriggled beneath them, annoyed. 'She *did* and if she's not been trying to hurt me and she's not bad, then . . . Well, what's it all been about? What does she want with me?'

Tarkus shook his head, and waved a hand to brush the question aside.

'This, all this is the business of the Older Powers. It's inadvisable for normal folk to meddle in their affairs. We just need to tell the Library and have done.'

'But why am I the only person Art has reached out to? That must mean something.'

He said nothing, but his burning eyes simmered with thought. Emily bit her lip. There was a memory, an idea, she couldn't stop coming back to.

'The faces, the hands . . . I think she's . . .' She'd almost got it. The anguished look on all the faces, and the grasping, imploring hands. Yes, she was sure of it. 'I think she's scared. Really scared but still reaching out,' Emily said.

'Scared?' He was looking at her as if she'd gone mad. 'She's terrifyingly powerful and clearly very angry and ready to lash out.'

'That's what happens when you're scared and lonely.'

She folded her arms across her chest.

'Really? How do you know?' he said in arch tones.

She just looked at him.

'Oh, I see,' he said, and stared at the carpet. Emily's mind was whirring furiously.

'All that beckoning and grabbing business . . .' Her brow was wrinkled with thought. 'Oh god, I think she wants to talk and I've been running away from her. I think she wants to tell me something.'

Tarkus had developed a finely honed sense for forthcoming plans that were likely to be wildly dangerous. The air around him filled with an eye-prickling reek of harsh ginger until the wind whipped it away.

'We need to find her. Straight away!' Emily thumped the carpet again and this time it bucked and they all came perilously close to falling off.

'Do you mind?!' shouted the pilot. 'She's very sensitive!'

'This is an extraordinarily bad idea,' said Tarkus, once he'd regained his seat. 'I thought you wanted to go straight to the Library, to tell her about the Nocturne's planned escape?'

Emily clenched her fists, torn.

'I do. We should . . . but this. I think it's important. It *is* important and we should find out what she wants first.' Her mind was made up. The resigned expression on Tarkus's face suggested that he knew it too.

'How do we find her? She just appears randomly. Generally at the most terrifying moment possible. Where do I start looking?' She was getting terribly flustered.

Tarkus reached out and touched her arm. 'When we first met, where did I say we would find the Library?'

'Eh?' said Emily, but she was already following on with the right answer. 'Where they keep all the books, of course. Oh, right!'

She smiled at him and he smiled back.

'Not bad, Watson, not bad. We'll make a detective of you yet.'

'I am already a detective,' he muttered, but his smile lingered.

'Okay, we've got a plan.' She whistled then shouted at the bolt-necked driver over the wind.

'Change of plan, Franky. Take us to the National Gallery instead.'

The carpet shifted and tilted as it changed direction, and they both had to hold on.

'It's the doctor who was called Frankenstein, you know,' came the muttered reply from the front of the rug.

'What?' shouted Emily.

'Never mind,' came the mournful voice. 'Never mind. Just forget it. Everybody else does.'

The gallery was closed, and the distinctly snooty many-armed curator had refused to let them in. Emily hadn't got her Library card, and he seemed unimpressed by Tarkus's Night Watch badge. In the end, Tarkus had been forced to whip out his Watch-issue hypno-mirror, and 'put the "fluence" on him'. Now the curator stood with a dreamy expression on his face, his many long arms all wriggling loose in the breeze.

'Are you sure that's like, ethical?'

Tarkus looked at the little mirror with affection.

'Oh yes, they're made by just one chap down on the Strand. Family business, I believe.'

'No, using it like that! I mean, look at Mr Tickle, he's all googly. Will he go back to normal?'

Tarkus paused and pursed his lips.

'Define "normal".'

'Man, you guys really need to invent health and safety.' Emily shook her head. 'Come on, we need to find the bit with the most art in.'

'I don't think that will be a problem,' said Tarkus, as they rounded the corner into the great hall. It was a massive, high-ceilinged room, lined completely with paintings: huge ones in vast gilt frames and smaller portraits dotted in between them. The central aisle was full of towering sculptures of bronze and stone. The room was a profusion of colour and form, and Emily didn't know where to look first.

'I brought my mother here when we first arrived, you know,' said Tarkus as he gazed around. 'She said it was one of the first signs of actual civilization she'd seen in the whole country.'

'Your mother sounds like punchy company,' Emily said.

He grinned. 'You have no idea. The thought of you two ever meeting is terrifying.'

She grinned back. The sweet smell of summer roses drifted between them, and she managed to forget how nervous she was for a moment.

'Right then, what do you think we should do? Go and knock on a painting?' She tugged Tarkus's cape. 'Do you think she's even here?'

A moaning, agonized creak of distressed metal filled the silent space. It came from the middle of the floor, where a couple forged from bronze broke off an intense snog they'd been locked in for a century and turned to face Emily and Tarkus. They didn't look particularly happy to be disturbed. That first movement was the domino that tumbled all the others and there was a chorus of metallic groans and gravelly noises of stone on stone as the whole row of statues turned to glare at them.

'Yes, I'm fairly certain she's here,' said Tarkus in a hoarse whisper.

All around them, the paintings jolted and started into life, a flare of colour and movement, a hundred TV screens set to different channels. Where there were figures, they came to the front of the frame and pressed themselves against it, all eyes turned towards Emily and Tarkus. There was not a sound in the whole hall apart from the thump of Emily's heart.

Tarkus took her arm.

'Are you sure about this? She is fearsomely powerful and we don't know if . . .' He gave a guilty start and leant to whisper in her ear. 'We don't know if she's gone mad.'

'I'm not even slightly sure, but I'm going to do it anyway. She saved me once. I have to try.'

Tarkus rubbed his hands together and pressed them to his mouth as he looked at the eerie occupants of the hall. The sharp menthol odour of camphor filled the air around him.

'You can stay here if you want. I know you're funny about the Powers,' she said.

He swallowed, then gripped his truncheon.

'Don't be ridiculous. I've wrestled a bear for you; I'm sure I can cope with some agitated portraiture.'

He squeezed her shoulder, and with that tiny warm contact she nearly couldn't do it. That little bit of safety reminded her she was absolutely bricking it, and the ever-watching eyes of the statues and paintings were making it worse. But then Emily thought of ignoring those silent screams before, of running from someone who was (she really really hoped) just scared, and knew she had to go on.

Emily ducked under the alabaster hand of a statue that had leant over to glare at her. Tarkus walked with her, and they edged down the gangway, turning this way and that to try and watch the artworks. As they walked, the silence was broken here and there by the creaking and grating of the statues all turning to watch them. On their right, the occupants of the paintings were pressed against the canvas like fish in a glass bowl, looking ready to break through into the world at any moment. Every eye in the place stared at her and she thought she might scream. Tarkus was breathing fast and his knuckles were white on his truncheon.

As they gingerly walked further in, there was a slow ripple of movement. Every arm and hand, whether painted or carved, was lifted, a silent Mexican wave of oil paints, marble and bronze that rose and fell, and left them all pointing in the same direction. The ones right by her were pointing in the direction they were headed, but the ones further on the aisle were pointing back towards them.

'They're all pointing *towards the same thing*,' Tarkus said.

Halfway down the hall was a particularly grand painting. It was hung in a huge gilt frame, and made the ones around it look like finger paintings. It showed a rickety horse-drawn cart in the middle of a shallow river near a little cottage. The paint was smeared thickly in places, then more delicately in others, and gave the most incredible sense of life and movement to the trees and the water, the cart and carters, and the dog on the bank of the river. It captured a glimpse of English summer and was quite wonderful. All the hands were pointed right at it. Unlike all the other paintings, it wasn't moving. It was perfectly still, as frozen as when it was painted.

Emily ducked under a bronze horse's pointing hoof and walked up to the painting. It really was big; the same height as her, and wider than it was tall.

'Erm . . . hello? I've come. That's what you wanted, right?'

Nothing. Not a sausage. The whole gallery was holding its breath and waiting. Not even slightly creepy, no sir.

'Art. You're Art, aren't you? I know you're friendly –' *Oh god, I hope you're friendly*, she thought – 'you warned me about the Bear, didn't you? Thanks for that.'

Still no movement, but there was . . . something. A distinct feeling that someone, some*thing*, was listening.

What was she meant to do?

'Erm . . . hello? Funny time to be shy, just saying, what with all the woo woo stuff before.'

Tarkus tutting echoed across the hall. She shot him a glare and tried again.

'I just . . . I'm sorry, I've been looking, and erm . . . running the other way, but I didn't understand.'

She got right up close to the painting, spotting other details; a little man fishing on the far bank, a lady washing clothes in the stream.

'I've come to you now, and there's no need to be scared.'

The hanging branches, draped down over the river, were moving ever so slightly now in the breeze. Wait, what breeze? Wind tousled her hair, and the scent of country air, and the delicate chuckle of water over stone and the creak of wooden wheels seeped out of the painting. The river was moving too, and dappled sunlight warmed her face through the leaves. She stared at it in amazement. A gentle summer's afternoon had opened up before her, and the picture was alive.

'Whoa, that's— Argh!'

She nearly jumped out of her skin. There was a woman standing on the grass in the left of the painting. She had absolutely not been there before, Emily would have sworn. The woman was looking at her. She was tall and painfully slender, dressed in an old-fashioned lacey white summer dress, with a white bonnet with flowers in, and a white parasol held unopened in one gloved hand. Her face was covered by a white veil that hung from the hat. She held herself at an awkward angle, her weight hunched to the side, and she was leaning on the parasol like a walking stick. Art had been badly injured in the War, the Library had said.

'Hello? Is that you?' she said. *Brilliant question, Emily. Top marks.* 'I mean, are you Art?'

The woman limped into the foreground of the painting. She took tiny fragile steps, like she was made of brittle glass. The painting flowed and remade itself around her and soon she was standing large in the foreground like someone come to a window. The detailed brush work grew ever finer as she did, and Emily leant in, fascinated. The veiled woman raised a white-gloved hand and gestured her closer.

'Be careful,' Tarkus said from behind her.

'What is it? What do you want to tell me?' said Emily, inching closer.

It was then the white-gloved hand shot out of the painting into the real world and grabbed the front of her hoodie. With a strangled chicken squawk, Emily was hauled face first into the painting.

CHAPTER 18

'Aaaaaargh!'

She'd expected to smack her nose on the canvas but instead she passed smoothly through it, *into* it. She stumbled to her knees on the grass-laced edges of a sandy river bank, the warm, lazy light of a summer's afternoon in rural Suffolk shining on her. The soft graze of grass on her hands was real, it had the sweetness of summer meadows, but there was just one thing...

'Cor, I'm all painty!' Any shock or fear was overwhelmed by the abrupt novelty. Emily held her hands up in wonder as she pushed herself back to her feet. 'Wow. Look at me.' She waved her hands in front of her face, and the tiny brushstrokes of paint moved to make up her painted self. As she lowered them, the woman in the white dress was standing right in front of her.

'Okay, really not cool! You need to ask before—'

She stopped as she saw the woman had her arm pressed in to her side and that leaning on the parasol was all that was keeping her upright. Emily's annoyance changed immediately to concern.

'Are you okay? Do you want to sit down?'

She offered an arm to the woman. To Art, rather. She was totally Art. Who else lived in a painting, and was pretty lanky and enigmatic, Library-style? Art, Older Power, creator of the Midnight Hour, and the third of the Sisters Three. Art leant upon her and, with the parasol as a cane and Emily's shoulder as a support, they hobbled to the clover and buttercup slope of the river bank by the old cottage. Emily had braced herself, but Art weighed next to nothing. There was the rustle of white lace, a waft of paint, and a curious throb of heat from her, but other than that there might just have been sticks in the dress. She was frail and brittle, and reminded Emily of her dad's mum, her old Nana Joan, not long before she died, all sparrow-light and dry, like a good wind could blow her away. By the time she had helped Art walk even that short distance Emily knew she wasn't well.

'Here we go.' She backed up and settled Art down on to

the soft grass, then plonked herself down next to her. Everything around her was fascinating. Ahead of them was the river, the laughing carters and their wagon and horses cooling off in it, and fine golden fields beyond. Yet off to the right was the frame of the painting. It hung in the air, a gilt-edged window into a dark blurred room, but around it was the painted world. The summer sun was warm, the grass was soft, and the water flowed by. It was a balm after the recent harried darkness of the Hour.

The painting's tiny brush strokes squirmed to fill the gaps as she looked around, but she found that if she moved her eyes around faster, the strokes weren't there when her eye first got there, only the blank ivory of an absence. The same colour as one of her mum's unused canvases. She was sat riverside, but it was only real here, at the heart of the painting. At the edges, the world started to fade. This didn't bother the little spaniel however, who trotted up, sniffed her hog-pocket, then stuck his furry painted head on her leg and immediately went to sleep.

Art sat more upright now. She leant towards Emily and her veil drew tighter on her face as she did. The shape beneath was fractured and reshaped in ways that faces usually weren't. Before Emily could move, the lace-gloved hand gently cupped her chin.

'Errrm . . . can I help you?'

Art did not speak, but turned Emily's chin left to right

and back again, angling her head from side to side. Art stared intensely at her, the unhealthy heat from her fingers warm on Emily's face. Or at least, Emily thought she was staring. There was a bright flickering glimmer of multi-coloured light pointed at her from beneath the veil. Art gave her the rainbow stare for a moment longer, then nodded, let go of Emily and leant back.

'So, that was weird. Look, what's going on? Why were you haunting me?'

Art's gloved fingers lifted up a locket on a chain from where it dangled on her chest (although Emily would have sworn it hadn't been there a minute ago). Her fingers twisted the clasp and popped it open. She dangled it out for Emily to see. Emily looked at the mini-portrait within, then looked again, eyes wide. The face was familiar, although the old-fashioned black lace dress and the normal-coloured hair were not.

'That's my mum! You know my mum?'

The picture had changed; now it was her mum, looking young and happy as she walked arm in arm with a tall woman in white whose face was concealed by shadows, although not her multicoloured eyes. The picture changed a few times without Emily seeing how it had, but in each one were two women of very different heights, looking happy together.

'Were you friends?'

Art's other hand crept up to touch her chest and she nodded.

As the pictures flickered in the locket, Emily could have sworn she saw one of her mum holding a hedgehog, but things were complicated enough without getting into that.

'So you're what, talking to me because of –' Emily flapped her hands – 'her?'

The tiniest of nods.

'Should have known it would be her fault.' She shook her head wearily. 'What do you want me to do?'

Art pointed at the picture of Maeve's face, then tapped the ground between them several times with the same finger, and nodded at Emily expectantly.

'You want me to get Mum to come here?'

Art nodded again, very definite this time. Emily groaned.

'Oh dude, this is very poor timing. She just can't.' Emily stuck her hands in her hoodie pocket and pouched it out so she looked preggo. 'She is way up the duff and mainly waddling.'

Art tilted her head sideways in puzzlement.

'I mean she won't come, just no way,' Emily said, shaking her head to make herself clear.

Art slumped like her strings had been cut. Emily grabbed for her hand.

'But I promise I'll help if I can. I'm a Librarian as well, like Mum was.' Emily squinted, puzzled. 'In fact, why haven't you just spoken to the Library? She's well worried about you.'

Art went rigid at the L-word. Above them, in the painted world, the summer sky darkened and thunder rumbled. Emily looked up, eyes wide. The skyscape full of gentle white summer clouds was transforming. The clouds were darkening and forming into two huge pillars of storm, that then became giant figures of women, as big as the sky. They were recognizable from their eyes – one pair as black as leaking ink, the other blue as the sky behind them. In between them was a smaller woman's figure made of white cloud, whose eyes were all the colours of the rainbow. The two thunderheads roared, both as terrible as the other, and the white cloud cowered, and the spaniel whined uneasily on Emily's knee.

'Are you saying you're scared of them— AARGH!'

There was a colossal bolt of lightning above so jarring that Emily bit her tongue. She couldn't have said which of the figures it came from, but the white cloud figure was shattered into a million tiny fragments of mist as the storm carried on. Art was staring at the floor.

'Oh god, was that what happened in the War? Wow, okay, that's pretty horrible.' She patted Art's arm gently; it was stick-thin beneath the lace. 'I don't know much about being a sister, well, not yet anyway, but I know the Library cares about you, she—'

There was another gigantic thunder crash overhead as Art stiffened, and the very ground shook.

'But I'm sensing some tension there, so let's move on, eh,' said Emily in a hurry.

As she spoke, the clouds returned to fluffy white status and the sun broke through and graced her skin with its warm touch again. Relaxing out in the river, one of the carters raised his hat at her, and she waved back.

'So . . . what did you want Mum for?' She shuffled around to look straight at Art. 'If you want to tell me, it might be easier if you, y'know, spoke.'

Art stayed unmoving and silent next to her.

'Wait, are you a not-talking-at-all person?' said Emily, cheeks burning. 'Because that's fine but it's going to make this more complicated.'

Art sat up straighter, and behind the veil her multi-coloured eyes flared brightly. She reached over and took Emily's hand. There was the rough-smooth finger touch of white lace, the desperately fragile brittleness beneath, and again that pulse of heat, far hotter than any normal skin. It reminded Emily of her furry hot-water-bottle dog, Spot. Art reached out and gestured at the air in front of them with her other white gloved hand. In an instant, part of the view of sun-drenched fields was scraped away, like wet paint with a pallet knife. Beneath the colours of the world was the ivory of a textured canvas.

Emily breathed as slowly as she could to calm her racing heart.

'Okay, so that's totally normal. This is how you're going to tell me?'

Art squeezed her hand.

'Ooh, idea! Squeeze once for yes, twice for no. Easy. We'll get this done in no time.'

Art gestured again and the blank canvas rapidly filled with colour, building up stroke by stroke, to create an oil painting of London. It was clearly the Midnight Hour version of London, as the moon hung huge in the sky, and Big Ben towered as a centrepiece, wreathed in the emerald arcs of magic light that rippled across it. The painting was hyper-realistic, very beautiful, and set in a solid frame of brass clockwork cogs. All of the clockwork was ticking in fluid motion.

'So, that's, like, meant to be the Midnight Hour, right? We've done metaphor in art class this year.'

Art didn't squeeze back to say yes, but she was staring at the painting with fierce concentration. There was a glitter of light from Big Ben, and a hole was punched out of the canvas near it, like a gunshot from the other side. Emily flinched back. Paint seeped out of it like blood from a wound.

'What—' Emily had started to ask, then other holes started to pepper the painting, circling the clock tower.

Each hole blew a piece of canvas out, and more and more paint started to leak out, pooling in the frame and dripping down. The Midnight London in the picture started to fade, the life leaking from it. The silver moonlight tarnished and the emerald magic faded to a jade ember. The clockwork frame snarled up as the paint ran into it and jammed the works. The whole thing was on the brink of collapse.

Then there was a final hole, blasted out straight above Big Ben. This one spilt out more gouts of paint, but something much worse too. As Emily watched horrified, bony, bandage-wrapped fingers started to unfold from inside the hole and grip the edges, like the legs of some terrible spider. Fingers all too like the ones she'd seen playing the organ earlier. They gripped the edges of the hole, then *ripped*. The painted clock tower was torn apart, the painting itself rent open across the middle, the frame shattered into fragments in a terrible silent explosion, and Midnight London was shredded into pieces.

Emily gasped. It woke the spaniel up, which ran away, barking.

'What . . . *what* was that? Is that what the Nocturne is going to do? This is what you wanted to tell Mum?'

A squeeze.

'Oh god. We've got to stop it. Can you help me?'

There wasn't a squeeze this time, but a tug. Art pulled

Emily towards her as she lifted her veil. Emily managed not to flinch, but it was difficult. Art's face was not so much ravaged as partly missing. Parts of her were there, and parts were not. The planes and geometries of symmetry were gone, leaving a badly done jigsaw of what had once been an alien beauty. Even through the shadows and holes and scarring, Art's expression was harrowed with grief. Art pointed to herself, to the parts of her that were missing, and shook her head.

She wasn't going to be helping anybody. Not like this.

CHAPTER 19

Emily exploded back out of the painting and stumbled as she found herself jumping down to floor level. She had to run to avoid falling flat on her face and crashed straight into Tarkus, who was standing nervously nearby.

'She pushed me in the river to send me home! That was totally uncalled for! Now I'm all wet!' She patted herself as Tarkus stared. 'Wait, I'm not wet at all!'

She gripped the rough fabric of his blue sleeves, her brain a firework display from all the mad things that had just happened.

'Oooh, paint magic!'

'Emily,' Tarkus said in his worried tone of voice.

'It's okay, I'm fine. She was fine. Nice even, but I need to tell you about the big picture – ha! – and the spider hands and—'

'Emily!' he spoke more urgently. He never normally used her name either. *Weird.*

'You're right, we need to go and find—'

'The Library!' he shouted, and grabbed her arm as he did.

'Exactly!' she said. He pinched the brow of his nose hard and she thought he was going to count to ten, but instead he just yanked her arm to turn her around.

'No, *the Library*,' he said quietly.

Looming right behind Emily, and hovering off the ground, was the Library. Her face was set in a grim mask, her long black hair floating out on unseen currents, eyes glistening as black ink flooded them. Emily had never seen the Library so intense, and that was saying something.

'*You have seen my sister?*' Her voice was a shriek, and echoed around the gallery.

Emily gulped.

'Yeah, she's right here in this . . .' She turned around to gesture at the painting she'd stumbled out of, but it was just a painting again. There was no white-veiled woman standing on the river bank. Emily looked this way and that as the Library's eyes burnt into her, but the gallery was totally still. It was full of art but Art was gone.

'Erm . . . I think she might have left already.' As she spoke the Library gusted past (she always forgot to walk when she was agitated, Emily had noticed) and ran her hands over the painting.

'How did she even get here?' Emily whispered to Tarkus.

'You were gone for a long time, and I was worried, particularly when the painting started rumbling, so . . . I wrote her a note.' The Library was instantly aware of any new writing in the Hour, Emily knew. 'Then she just appeared and started screeching at me. I think she's having one of her—' He stopped talking as the Library glided back to them.

'What did she say? What is her condition? Tell me!'

The Library was right up close, meaning Emily had to look up at a neck-craning angle. The Library's eyes were brimming with black ink – a sign she might be about to get lost in the words that sometimes overwhelmed her.

'She didn't *say* anything. She'd be great at Pictionary though.' The Library's mad-eyed stare suggested this was more info than she needed. 'Uh, but she showed me something awful.'

Emily started to sketch out a giant frame-shape with her hands. 'So, the Midnight Hour is a big painting with holes in and all the paint will pour out through the holes soon, particularly if the big spider hands come out and pull it apart.'

She did the 'spider hands pulling the Hour apart' gesture, but it didn't help the look of incomprehension on both the Library and Tarkus's faces.

'Don't look at me like that! It's really hard talking about a conversation you had in a vision.'

Emily concentrated and told them everything about Art and what she had been shown inside the picture. She also told the Library about the Nocturne. She didn't get into Art's feelings about the Library though. It didn't feel like a good time to bring it up.

The Library closed her eyes and tensed her hands, locked in a battle of will with herself. Her feet touched down on the floor and her hair settled back on her shoulders. Her skin glowed like polished wood and she might have been carved until she opened her now-clear eyes and spoke.

'My sister has been partly restored by the flow of new art from the Daylight realm. Even as the Nocturne works to destroy all we have built, she brings back the one I care for more than anything . . .'

She smiled but there was no humour in it at all.

'. . . just in time to see everything we created ruined. Art warns us that my other sister will not merely escape through this twelfth Hole she speaks of, but will destroy the Hour with it as she does.'

'Okay, that's extraordinarily heavy,' said Emily.

Tarkus put his face in his hands.

'Then we do not have long. My family do not have long.' He stared unblinking at the Library. 'What can we do to save this world, Great Lady? What will *you* do?'

'I . . . I am at a loss,' said the Library.

'*What?!*' yelled Tarkus, then clapped his hand over his mouth.

'But you're like the most grown-up grown-up I know,' said Emily. 'You must have a plan. Tell us what to do!'

The Library's toes were starting to lift off the floor again.

'This Hole is worse than I imagined. It must be found and closed before the Nocturne destroys the whole Hour with it, and yet –' her eyes bloomed afresh with blots of ink – 'Art was the architect of the Great Working. I would need her help to close a breach of this size and . . . and she . . . has not . . .' She faltered then spoke in as small a voice as Emily had ever heard her use. 'Why didn't she come to me instead?'

Aw man.

'Erm, well, this is major awks, but I think she's kind of . . . scared of you after what happened in the War?'

The Library's face contorted.

'But mainly of the Nocturne!' Emily added hurriedly. 'Look, what did happen—'

The Library threw herself back to her full height, her

hair lashing out and her eyes flashing black. Emily cringed as she waited for a colossal freak-out, then . . . a sound cut between them, a wracking, heaving cry of pain. The Library had sobbed. She put her head forward and her hair fell over her face, and black inky tears splashed on to the floor. Emily and Tarkus looked at each other. What do you do when semi-omnipotent beings start ugly-crying in public?

'Farewell happy fields, Where joy forever dwells: Hail, horrors, hail,' The Library chanted from beneath her tidal wave of hair. 'The Nocturne struck the blow but I made Art tread the battlefield.'

'Great Lady,' said Tarkus in a loud voice, talking over the Library. She raised her head and gave him a look that would have set most people on fire, but Tarkus's eyes were already blazing with anger. 'This is about all of our families, not just yours. Please, you need to help us. Your sister needs to help us too.'

The Library's voice was like echoes from a dark well.

'We have been together for aeons of time your limited minds cannot even comprehend, and now you tell me that she is scared of me?' The ink tears were rolling freely down her cheeks in black streams. 'Making my sister help you all is what caused this. I will not put her in harm's way again. I will not.'

She floated upwards, eyes full of blackness and hair

adrift in an invisible ocean. When Emily had first met her the Library had not been very stable, and these were all the signs of a major book-wobble coming.

'Okay, calm down, we really need you to focus on this whole Hole thing.'

The Library spun in the air, her hair a cloud around her, a doomed drowned ballerina in tattered lace. She might have been in the same room but she was clearly somewhere else in her head.

'Things fall apart; the centre cannot hold. I must find her. Ask her forgiveness. Protect her.'

'Great Lady, no!'

'Oh, please don't do this now. Come on, we need to—'

It was too late. The Library drifted across the room, as if gravity only happened to other people, and away through the statues and out of sight. She never once looked back.

'Firstly,' said Emily in the consequent silence, 'I think that the "limited minds" thing was out of order.' She bit her knuckle hard, leaving white marks. 'Secondly, it's happening again, isn't it?'

'What?' said Tarkus.

'I'm— I mean, *we're* going to have to come up with a plan and save the world.' She sighed. 'This is totally unreasonable. I already have homework.'

'There must be someone else who can help? We cannot just . . .' The air around Tarkus was filled with the thick smell of sage as he wrung his hands together.

'Can you honestly think of anybody, apart from maybe my mum and dad . . .' Emily winced at the thought of them. She was in so much trouble. 'Apart from them, who would have the foggiest how to try and sort this out?'

Tarkus's face writhed as he rocked in thought, then settled into a form of calm anguish. The sage clarified to a more piney smell that put Emily in mind of winter forests.

'No, I cannot. Even the sarge has gone off to be pruned.' Tarkus's sergeant, as well as being two feet tall, was made of ivy. He sighed and squared his shoulders. 'It seems the bad-luck vortex and the brilliant detective—'

'Assistant detective,' Emily butted in.

' . . . must solve another undoubtedly life-threatening and hideously unpleasant case.'

'Too right, and there's only one thing to do at a time like this.' She punched him in the arm and spoke in the sonorous tones of one quoting great wisdom. '*When in doubt, make a list*. Hand over your pad, pinefresh.'

Tarkus fished his official notepad out of his cloak, along with a pencil, and despite Emily grasping for them, sat down on the base of a statue, and poised himself to take dictation.

'I'll do the writing, it's an official Night Watch pad.'

'Very good, Watson.' She began to pace and wished she had a pipe or a violin or whatever it was great detectives did while they were cracking cases.

'Right, this needs a two-column list to start; things we know and things we don't know.'

Tarkus looked up. 'Hadn't we better include things we don't know we don't know too?'

'What?! What are they?'

'*I don't know*, obviously, but if there's something we don't know about and we don't find out about until too late, then it could all go horribly wrong.'

'Oh, that's great. Very cheering. Please stop helping.' She began to pace again. 'We don't know where the Hole is going, particularly where the twelfth location is, and we have to find out.'

He scribbled as she spoke.

'And if we did know, we don't know how to close it.' She paused and bit her lip. 'I've seen Art close up, and there's no way she can do it. She nearly collapsed just getting me into the painting.'

She paused in thought. 'That's . . . that's the main ones.'

Tarkus nodded as he gazed at the pad.

DON'T KNOWS
HOLE - LOCATION (12th VERY IMPORTANT)
HOLE - CLOSING, HOW TO (PRE-APOCALYPSE)

'That's a short list. I thought you didn't know lots more things than that.'

She screwed her face up at him. 'Cheers. It might be short but it is basically impossible.'

'Reminds me of somebody I know.'

She nodded in appreciation. Despair was filling him with zingers. 'Right. Next list. What do we know?'

'Start with the Hole,' he said. 'It's the most important.'

She stared vacantly into the middle distance as she summoned up all the facts. 'Well, the Hole moves around London, and stops in different places for a while. It comes out in the same place in the Daylight as it is here.' She thought about the Bearskins and winced. 'Pretty much, anyway . . .'

'Okay. What do we know about how it moves?' Tarkus scribbled without looking up.

'Well, it's getting faster, apparently. Its orbit is speeding up, the Nocturne said, or something like that anyway, and when it gets to the twelfth Hole the Hour's doomed.'

They were both quiet for a moment.

'We must figure out where it's going.' Tarkus frowned at the pad as if he could make it confess. 'You said earlier that only the "idiot-faced Pooka, Bronflakes" knows where it will go?'

Emily grinned. 'Exactly.' Her grin faded. 'Well, that's not totally right. Brongo was getting her deets from the Nocturne.'

'So the Nocturne knows where the Hole goes?'

'Yeah, she'd got a map of London and was working out where it would go next.'

'You saw it?' Tarkus leant in, intent.

She shook her head. 'No, only for a moment. She was working stuff out with one of them two-pointy things for drawing circles.'

'A compass?'

'That's the one.'

'So she was plotting something.' His eyes lit up. Literally.

'She's always plotting something! How does that help?'

He bit his lip and closed his flaming eyes.

'I mean,' he said after a pause in which he appeared to be counting silently, 'that she was plotting something out on the map. Which means the movement of the Hole is predictable. It's not random magic.'

'Ohhhh!'

'Now, we know more than we did. We know some of the places the Hole stopped too.'

'Oh yeah! I came back in at Buckingham Palace, and the Nocturne sent Bron out to St James's Palace for the next stop.' She pressed hard at her temples to try and squeeze more information out. 'Mammy said the first one . . . was outside Somerset House. That's it though, all I've got.'

'That's not it.' Tarkus flicked back through the pages in his notepad. 'Let's see, you have previously mentioned that

Pat named a Hole at Bedlam hospital and "Brongle" indicated there was one in the middle of the river near Vauxhall.'

'That's brilliant!' Emily clapped. 'Hang on, do you write down everything I say?'

'Only the useful bits. It's another very short list.'

'Oi.'

'So, we have five Holes. We must divine the damn thing's path from that. We need a map.' He stood up. 'Come on. I know just the place.'

'Oh! You know what this means?'

'What?'

'Research montage!'

He shook his head. 'I'm so glad the fate of my world is in your hands.'

CHAPTER 20

A power walk along bustling pavements later, they were in the vast, domed silence of the British Museum reading room. This was the Library's usual home and it felt empty without her drifting presence amongst the towering shelves. Standing at a table lit by hastily gathered gas lamps, Tarkus struggled to unroll a massive map. The map was clearly enchanted; lights dotted it and the Thames was flowing (which had the unfortunate side effect of making Emily need a wee). Tarkus winced as Emily grabbed what were probably priceless first editions to use as paperweights for three of the corners. She used Hoggins for the fourth one, and he was still snoring as she popped him down.

'Right, let's mark the places the Hole has been. List please, Watson.'

DO-KNOWS
HOLE SPEEDING UP
WORLD ENDS AT TWELFTH STOP
MOVEMENT NOT RANDOM
KNOWN HOLE LOCATIONS:
BUCKINGHAM PALACE
ST JAMES'S PALACE (PALACE CONNECTION?)
BEDLAM HOSPITAL, SOUTHWARK
SOMERSET HOUSE
RIVER (MIDDLE), NR VAUXHALL

She reached over with a pencil to circle Buckingham Palace on the map but he grabbed her wrist, and instead marked the spot with a small coin from his pocket. She stuck her tongue out at him as he read from the pad and pointed.

'Somerset House.'

He glared at the pencil she was still wielding, so she dug into the pocket of her joggers and pulled out half a biscuit.

'Ooh, I've been looking for that.' She bit it in half again, and popped it down to mark the spot. The remaining three were marked with a stone out of her trainer treads, a half-chewed tulip bulb from Tarkus's snack pocket and a significant-sized ball of fluff from Emily's joggers. They gazed at their motley little bunch of things clustered on the map. Tarkus reluctantly said what they were both thinking.

'There's no pattern. It's vaguely central but appears on both sides of the river and in no apparent shape. It's just random.'

There was a faint odour of mothballs in the air by him, and he was frowning so hard Emily was concerned he'd stick like it. She had to admit she couldn't see any pattern either. She gnawed her lip.

'In the films, if you plot stuff on the map then draw lines through it, it normally shows up as a pentangle.'

'Pentacle,' said Tarkus wearily.

'Whatever, Mr Clever. A pentacangle where the terrible ritual is going to take place and the tentacles are going to come out, or whatever.'

Tarkus's eyebrows shot up in alarm.

'You think there'll be a tentacle issue? I do have a page on that in the handbook somewhere.' He was already rooting in his uniform pocket.

'No! It was an example. But I don't even know where to start with drawing lines between these.' She glared at the markers. 'They're all over the place.'

Tarkus put his hands on the top of his Night Watch helmet and pressed it down over his eyes. The distinct odour of rotting veg filled the air around him.

'Calm down, compost. I need your brain on this,' said Emily.

'This helps me think,' he said in a muffled way from under the helmet. 'It occurs to me it would not in fact be that shape, because the Hole stopped at other places. We just don't know where they were.'

She stared at the map. 'That's . . . actually a really good point.'

'The final Hole is the twelfth, according to the Nocturne, so there are another seven,' he said, pulling his helmet up and off with a grunt. His pointy ears sproinged out as he did.

'So we're missing loads.' She scratched her head, her brain full of grit. 'I think that actually makes it worse. How are we supposed to— *Hoggins*, that is not helping!'

He had snoozily bumbled over from his important paperweight job to chew contentedly on Somerset House, or at least the quarter of a biscuit that marked it. She leant over to scoop him up and he rolled into a spiky ball to defend his biscuit. From directly overhead his perfectly spherical little body filled the space between the markers, touching all of them. She gave a sharp intake of breath. Tarkus leant in, rapt with attention.

'What have you see—'

'Shhhh!' She held up a finger to stop him talking. 'Big shush. Big thoughts. Thinking.'

He waved his hands in annoyance, but did, helpfully, shut up. Emily's mind was racing. She studied the Hog-map, brow furrowed, chin resting on her fist in her pose of ultimate concentration. She bonked herself repeatedly on the head with the pencil as her brain went into overdrive.

'The Nocturne said the Hole's orbit was speeding up. An orbit goes round something, right?' She didn't wait for a reply. 'And she had a compass, which draws circles and . . . What if they go all round the hedgehog?'

Tarkus looked at her blankly.

'I mean, what if the Hole is moving in a circle?'

She gently scooped an unrolled Hoggins up then showed Tarkus by moving her finger around the imagined circle edge where he had been. It connected each of the spots.

'See! It is. Good Hoggins, you may now eat Somerset House.' She rubbed his little nose. 'Although you must cut back on the biscuits or you will turn into a hedgepodge.'

'You have cracked it. I am sure the other stops are on this track.' Tarkus beamed with relief. 'So, if it's an orbit, what are they orbiting? The middle is exactly . . . here. Oh sweet Hecate.'

His beaming smile faded, as he looked at the green light flickering from the centre of the circle on the enchanted map.

'Oh man. Not Big Ben again,' groaned Emily.

They shared a haunted glance.

'So that's the twelfth Hole.' Tarkus turned to the door. 'We must alert the sorcerers while we still can.'

'But that's . . . It's just . . . that doesn't feel right.' Emily stayed staring at the map. 'Why would it be in the middle, when the rest are round the outside?'

Tarkus stared at her, not speaking, his eyes tiny furnaces.

'"Like clockwork". That's what Pat said. The Hole moves on like clockwork.' She scrunched her face up in thought. 'I can almost see it. How does the whole Hole clock clockwork work?' She paused. 'God, try that three times fast.'

She circled her finger around and around over the map, tracing the circle.

'It's speeding up, the Nocturne said, as magic gets out and time gets in, clockwork goes faster, clocks, time, midnight— Oh, bloomin' heck! That's it!' She belted herself on the head with the pencil again.

'Oh, I'm a stupid in the head stupid. Art tried to show me already. She even put Big Ben in the middle!'

She practically hovered over the map as she pointed.

'It *is* clockwork! It's a clockface! Big Ben is the centre, but the Hole is ticking around the hours! There *are* twelve. Every place the Hole has stopped has been at one of the hours on the clock face. Look!'

Tarkus's eyes were flaming enough to cast shadows.

'I think you are right.'

They grinned madly at each other with elation, gabbling as they both pointed at the map.

'This is the first one, Somerset House at one o'clock, Bedlam at four, the river at six, then Buckingham Palace at nine.' Tarkus tapped the map as he spoke.

'So that was the last stop where I came in, and Bron's next location in St James's is exactly where ten o'clock should be. That proves it!' she squealed.

'So the eleven o' clock Hole about here . . . in Piccadilly Circus?' Tarkus poked the map. 'And the twelfth one, the midnight one, here, directly north of Big Ben?'

'Where is it?'

He lifted his finger. 'Coven Gardens.'

'Covent Garden, you mean?'

'No, no, definitely *Coven*. It's where the witches grow their potion ingredients.'

'Whatever it's called, that's it, the twelfth Hole, I'd bet my last jammy dodger on it.'

'Your jam is safe. I concur.' He rubbed his chin. 'I would also wager my remaining tulip bulb that if it's tied to the Great Working, then the twelfth Hole will open at midnight, Daylight time.' He flicked open his night watch and they both looked at the miniature Big Ben's dials.

'If that's the case, we don't have long,' said Emily.

The brief joy left Tarkus's face like a light being flicked

off. 'Our other problem still stands. How are we supposed to close the Hole?'

'I don't know.' Emily put her head in her arms on the table. All she could think of were the spider fingers coming through the painting to rip the world apart.

'I'd normally make another list of things that could help, but I'm not sure I've got anything to put on it.'

'Well, you've got me,' said Tarkus.

Emily peeked over her arms.

'True.' She sat up. 'And humble though you may be, that is at least something.'

'Charming,' Tarkus grumbled, but they shared a smile.

'Right, my turn with the pad. It's brainstorm time. We can do this. In fact, we *have* to.'

After Tarkus reluctantly handed the pad over, some serious scribbling followed, along with a lot of muttering.

'Got the scary lady here, the Holey there. No, won't work. Art could do it but she's all wonky. What if we went to, nope, no time. I could invent machine guns? No, still no time. Better cross out "roller skates" too. If only we could get some— Ooh . . .'

Her tongue inched out of the corner of her mouth as she lost herself in thought. Tarkus peered at the tangled web of words, balloons and arrows, then jumped back in alarm as Emily reared up with a yell.

'I'm a genius!'

'What is it?'

'It's easy, I've got a way to fix everything. I'm going to send . . . no, no!' She slammed her hand on the table. 'It doesn't work!'

'Why? What, even?'

'I need someone to go to the Daylight but even with your stupid egret key they can't get out until exactly midnight.' She slumped back on to the table again. 'It's ruined, my plan doesn't work unless we can leave the Hour before the twelfth Hole opens, but we can't.'

'That's not entirely true,' Tarkus said.

She glared at him.

'Don't make me stab you with this pencil.'

Tarkus rolled his eyes. 'We *can* get out before midnight. The Hole is open all the time. And we know where the tenth, eleventh, and twelfth stops are. Probably.'

'Oh my god, I could kiss you.'

He stiffened in horror. 'I'd really rather you didn't.'

She rolled her eyes back at him.

'Anyway, that's brilliant. I'm glad my inspiring leadership has been having a formative effect on you.'

'But—'

'No time to thank me now. I know exactly how to use this breakthrough.'

'What are you going to do?'

She paused and a wide, incredulous grin spread over her

face. 'I am actually getting the gang back together for one last heist. Who'd have thought it?'

'Explain yourself, woman,' Tarkus folded his arms across his chest, 'before I snap and make you smell of bin juice for ever.'

'Come along, Watson, the game's afoot!' She scooped the Hog up into her pocket, then marched past him. 'I'll tell you on the way to the Coach and Horses.'

'What? Why are we going there?' He was spinning around in the backdraught of Hurricane Emily.

'I'm planning a criminal conspiracy. Best not to worry about it.' She sucked air through her teeth as something occurred to her. 'Y'know, there is one other minor niggle . . .'

He stared at her, mouth open, and held up his hands. *What?*

'We're going to need to do something stupidly dangerous to stop the Nocturne destroying the world before this genius plan can take effect.'

'Oh good,' said the long-suffering policeman.

CHAPTER 21

And so Emily and Tarkus had hurtled through London again, silver-kissed by moonlight. A hectic headlong pelt through snarled streets to the back room of a public house of ill-repute in Soho. Here she told her plan to a dark smoke-filled corner that might have been empty if it wasn't for the glint of a single red eye. A plan that would cross worlds, build bridges, and involve telling some terrible fibs. With that done it only remained to run further into the night to face the very worst, with nothing but hope and a hedgehog.

They were both breathing hard by the time they got near to Coven Gardens. Fog filled the streets here. A pea-souper frozen in time by the unchanging weather and covering all in a thick yellowish blanket of sound-dampening cotton wool. Emily had to hold on to Tarkus's blue cape to not lose him in the smog. Blinded by the fog as she was, she felt the gardens before she saw them. The ground under her feet changed from harsh stone cobbles to soft and yielding moss. She was looking down at this unexpected green when they stepped out into clear air. The fog stopped at the edge of Coven Gardens as if it had been sliced off with a knife, and it revealed something wondrous.

In her London, Covent Garden was hectic, crowded with shoppers hustling into the market buildings and tourists watching serious street entertainers outside. Not just some bloke and a guitar but circus acts and stage magicians and acrobats. It was always a noisy riot. Here, it was ... different.

They were standing, looking out over what should have been the wide paved area, the piazza, that sat in between St Paul's Church on the left and the huge market buildings on the right. But here, in Coven Gardens, the piazza wasn't paved, it was thick grass and moss and flower beds and plantings and fruit and fungi and bushes and trees. Here it *was* a garden. It wasn't just the piazza either; everywhere here was filled with life. On the left, the simple squared shape and peaked roof of St Paul's Church was totally green. The tall pillars on the porch at the front were invisible beneath the climbing vines that had wrapped themselves around them and spiralled up to the roof and turned them emerald. The walls and gates to its own churchyard were enmeshed in growth, night-blooming roses and a wildness of thorns.

Opposite St Paul's, across the piazza, lay the giant glass-roofed buildings of the market. In Emily's time they were full of posh shops and had, before that, been one of the busiest markets in London. Now, here in this moon-touched world, they were instead greenhouses, hanging gardens, vast terrariums. Greenery grew up and over them, and inside they burgeoned full of an exotic throb of plant life and fragrance and colour.

Above the piazza, floating globes of witchlight bobbed here and there, casting a softer light than the moon's sometimes harsh glare and bringing out the richness of colour that was all around. A distinctly low leaden-coloured cloud hovered around slowly, showering rain on each section of the garden at a time. Apart from witchlight and rain clouds, the other main thing that hung in the air was silence. Between the dampening effect of the surrounding fog and the insulation of everything being covered in leaves or moss or blades of grass, hardly a sound could be heard. After the roar and mayhem of getting across London, it was an oasis. Others clearly thought so too; there were

Night Folk all through the gardens.

Bearded women in robes balanced precariously on stepladders and trimmed mistletoe from trees with gleaming scythes. Young squid-headed lovers, chin tentacles entwined, strolled about and soaked up the rain from the mobile cloud. Ogre nannies and lunching office goblins sat on stone benches and took the air. A meeting of the pointy hat gardening club, all black capes and brooms and pointing at poisonous plants, pottered round the greenhouses. The place quietly bustled and was filled with calm and kindness. It seemed an unlikely place for the end of the world.

'This is brilliant, *brilliant*. Why have you never told me about this?'

'Hmmm? It's just the Coven Gardens.' Tarkus was distracted, scanning the gardens for Holes and arch-villains. 'I come here for my twelveses sometimes.'

Emily was still staring bug-eyed at it all, and he smiled at her, the tension leaving his face.

'It is charming, isn't it? Anyone in the community can prune whatever they need for their potions.' He tugged her arm. 'Come on, we need to look around anyway and there's something I need to do.'

They walked a circuit of the gardens and Tarkus began snapping off every handy flower head or glowing berry they passed, forcing them down as fast as he could. His expression suggested he wasn't enjoying it either. As they passed through the mushroom meadow, he dropped to his knees and began jamming bright red-and-white capped fungi into his mouth.

'I'm a big fan of snack attacks, but this is not the time. We need to find the Hole,' said Emily.

'This is exactly the time. It might be life-saving,' he said around a mouthful of 'shroom.

'Well, I'm starving too. I didn't get my running waffle and you know that imminent apocalypses make me hungry.' She cast around and spotted a likely treat glistening on a nearby branch. 'Ooh, berries!'

He grabbed her hand as she reached for them. 'I really wouldn't. We're in the poison garden.'

She pulled back and then watched in shock as he plucked a bunch himself and starting chewing them and spitting the seeds out.

'I thought you said—'

'They are. It's different for ghûls.'

'They better be. Berry-hogger.'

Their path had taken them on a full circuit and they were over by the market greenhouses, close to where they had come in. They had seen every magical plant in the world. What they hadn't seen yet, though, was the Hole.

'What if I've got it wrong?' she said. 'What if it's happening somewhere else?'

Tarkus pointed. 'Look!'

It was difficult to see against the foggy backdrop but, on the far side of the piazza, a flickering spinning golden hoop had drifted into the gardens and was sliding across the grass. It was the Hole.

It glided along on an arced path and stopped nearly opposite them, right in front of the overgrown doors of St Paul's, under the vast green-pillared portico. The edges of the Hole crackled and flashed in a Catherine-wheel flicker of sparks that reflected off the damp ivy leaves. It had slid in without anyone seeing it, but when it sucked in a passing giant moth with a bug-zapper crackle, leaf-clipping priest-esses started nudging each other and moving away.

It was bigger than before, and more potent. It had spread out to the size of a train tunnel. A prickly feeling of static crackled from it, even as far away as they were. That, and the glitchy glinting of the rim, gave her the uncomfortable sensation of standing too close to an uncaged tiger.

'Oh Hecate, you were right,' Tarkus said in a low voice.

'No need to sound so surprised.'

'This isn't surprise, it's terror.' He'd gone pale again. 'You were right, which means *She* is coming.'

Emily gulped.

'I do wonder whether we should have involved the rest of the Night Watch,' said Tarkus.

'So she can just music them all so they do what she

wants?' She glared at him. 'That reminds me, have you got your wax ready?'

He held out his hand to show her two thick plugs of soft white tallow wax that he was going to jam into his ears to keep the Nocturne's power at bay.

Doubt flooded her again. This was all so big and she was so small. What had she been thinking? 'Maybe, with more of that wax we could get some—'

'Too late,' he said, and gripped her arm so hard it hurt.

Awful, dimly seen figures were emerging from the fog on the far side of the piazza. An indistinct, hulking shadow at first, then another shape, taller than the first, with four legs and red eyes and a mound atop with glints of sapphire blue. As they strode out of the miasma and into the witch-light, all became clear. At the front, the terrible mass of the Bear, walking on two legs in his three-quarters bear form, all fur and muscle and killing claws, but wearing his hideously distorted human face. Behind him, a big black horse, with flaring mane, mad red eyes and white foam around the mouth. On its back sat the Nocturne. She was not the terrifying power Emily had faced before at the top of Big Ben, but her back was straight and her hair was sable, and although she still wore the half-mask, there was a blue furnace gleam from her eyes. With her came a faint sound of distant music, at the edge of hearing.

The Bear held a paw out for the Nocturne, and she

dismounted. As she did, the horse flickered out of existence, and was replaced with Bronagh, hair pinned up at the sides into a flowing red mane, black make-up slashed under each eye and down her cheeks, and draped in leather and a cloak of black feathers. She looked, Emily hated to admit, like some kind of war goddess. Together, the three of them stood and surveyed the gardens. Bron pointed at the Hole, grinning. Tarkus's grip on Emily's arm grew tighter.

'I thought you said she was withered and powerless? She does not look withered.'

'She was like a prune on a stick, I swear. That is some kind of makeover. Bron must have brought a load of new music in.' She scowled. 'She's still not final boss level though. We've got a chance. Probably.'

Now, as the villains started across the piazza towards the Hole, a ripple of movement passed through the gardens. Nannies gathered up their litters of pups. Office workers folded papers and briskly strode away, looking at their pocket watches. Druidesses left their stepladders without looking back. It was like an end-of-lunchtime bell had been rung and everyone was leaving. It seemed bad news travelled fast. The gardens emptied and left Emily and Tarkus standing alone, watching a nightmare approach.

'How did we imagine we could beat them?' said Tarkus. He had let go of her arm and drawn his truncheon out of his belt loop.

'We don't have to. We just need to stop them ripping the Hole wide open for as long as we can.' Emily let out a deep breath. 'I'm going to use my superpower of being really annoying.'

Tarkus nodded. 'That could work. You are extraordinarily annoying.'

She elbowed him but was actually quite pleased. 'Oh god, here they come. Are you sure you want to handle the Bear again?'

'I'm the closest thing we have to an expert.' He smiled thinly as he held up his silver whistle. 'Are you ready?'

'Absolutely not.'

'Me neither,' he said, and blew the whistle as hard as he could as they marched straight out to meet terror head-on. As the whistle continued to blow, the Bear raised one vast hairy paw to his ear and shook his head angrily. Bron snarled. The Nocturne scowled at the discord. She raised a bandaged hand, pinched her fingers together and twisted, like snapping a fly out of the air. As she did, Tarkus's whistle faltered and squeaked off into silence. He blew harder, but no noise came out.

'Well, well, if it isn't Hairy Potter and Bron Weasley,' said Emily. 'And Lord Holedemor— Nah, needs work. Anyway, look at the state of you lot.'

The Nocturne barely looked at them.

'Ursus, deal with them and redeem yourself. Bronagh,

attend me.'

The Bear's teeth gleamed as he strode towards them, his vast bulk cutting them off. The Nocturne ignored them and continued across the gardens to the Hole.

'Tiny meat snacks!' The Bear grinned at Emily from a face that glistened with cuts and scratches. His nose was horribly mangled after colliding with both the door and Mammy's teeth. 'Good. Was peckish.'

Tarkus gestured Emily back behind him.

'I, Tarkus Poswa, Provisional Inspector in charge of Doors, Portals, Gates and other Means of Egress, am ordering you to move away from the illegal dimensional cavity, or I shall have to arrest you.'

'Had this talk before, boy. Didn't go well for you.'

'Didn't go well for me? I seem to remember you falling down a very long drop and hitting every landing on the way down.' Tarkus smiled as the Bear snarled.

'Enough talk. Bear eat you now.' He reared up to his full height, casting a long shadow over the young policeman.

'Eat this instead.'

With a flick of his hand, and a flare of his eyes that lit the whole area up like a firework, Tarkus blasted the Bear and his oh-so-sensitive nose with the combined force of every bizarre aromatic, poisonous and magical herb he'd been forcing down himself since they got here. A more potent sorcerous brew couldn't be imagined; it was full of nightshade and mandrake, hemlock and hexweed, destroy-ing angel and fly agaric, as much poison as potion. Emily was well behind him and her eyes still stung and her nose burnt and she choked out a cough as her throat tightened. She couldn't imagine how the Bear felt.

The Bear wobbled, tottered, then straightened up. His fur was bleached where the blast had hit and his eyes were red but, apparently, otherwise he felt just fine. Tarkus's eyes widened in horror as the Bear roared with laughter, vicious white teeth the size of kitchen knives clashing around his giant pink tongue.

'Unlucky. Another day maybe but –' he rubbed a razor-tipped paw along his battered, swollen, shredded snout – 'Bear have big nose problem. No smelling. Big problem for you too. But not for long.'

'Oh dear,' said Tarkus in a very tiny voice, and started to scrabble in his jacket. As he did the Bear reared up to his full height, surged forwards and slammed down on top of him. Emily screamed and looked away. However, when no terrible sounds of rending flesh or chewing followed, just a loud purring noise, Emily forced herself to look. She saw Tarkus crouched down with the vast furry tsunami of the Bear curved over him but not touching. Tarkus was hold-ing something over his head like a shield, right in front of the Bear's muzzle.

It was the small silver hypno-mirror. The surface of the

mirror was spinning in a whirlpool of silver and furry brown reflection. The Bear was swaying in place, drool pooling on his lolling tongue and dripping off his awful teeth, his eyes rolling and vacant as he purred. All his attention was locked on the mirror.

Tarkus cracked an eye open and looked up at his hand, surprised it was still attached. Seeing the Bear frozen, he stood up straighter, keeping the mirror very carefully positioned in front of the Bear's eyes.

'I didn't think that was going to work,' he said, and swiped off the sweat that had appeared on his brow. 'Erm, right, you are under my command and will do exactly as I say. You are under arrest for the crime of tampering with the sovereign borders of the Midnight Hour, and being despicably hairy.'

The Bear moaned and staggered to the side. Tarkus had to do a fast two-step to keep the mirror in front of him.

'I have no idea if this will last,' he gasped at Emily. 'You have to stop them!'

The Bear reeled off through the green curtain of the sweeping fronds of a willow tree, and Tarkus had no choice but to go with him. They vanished from view, leaving Emily alone watching the Nocturne and Bron as they neared the Hole where it sat glistening in the shadow of the portico.

She ran over, shouting.

'Oi, you pair, the Watch is coming, and they've got earplugs and—'

Before she'd finished, Bron was already stalking back to meet her. The Nocturne didn't even turn to look.

'Why won't ye take a hint, half-breed? Ye're not wanted here,' Bron snarled. Her eyes were glowing full Pooka-red and there was a hint of wolfishness about her face already. 'I'm going to teach ye for interfering.'

'Why are you doing this? You'll destroy the world! Everyone will fade away, including the Pooka.'

Bron had still not closed the gap between them. She bristled and shook her finger at Emily.

'That's not so. The Lady's chosen will still have the magic and we'll be free.'

'Oh god, you've let her into your head, haven't you?' Emily eyed Bron up, remembering the seductive, haunting music that had played in her own ears when she'd met the Nocturne. 'You can't trust her. She tells the truth, but only the bits that help her. She tricked me then tried to kill me and my mum!'

Bronagh flinched, her eyes faded back from red to their shimmering green, and Emily knew she had reached her. Then the music that had been playing just on the cusp of hearing picked up to a louder volume, from the buzzing of a fly to too-loud earphones level. Bron shook her head, her hair flailing, and groaned in anguish.

'No! It's the right thing I'm doing. This is my destiny and you're in the way.'

Under her waterfall of hair (such great hair) there was a flicker of red light. Bron growled and it wasn't a human noise at all. Her hands were already lengthening into claw-tipped paws. Emily took a step back. Distraction Chat 101 had failed. Behind Bron, the Nocturne had turned to watch, her terrible half-grin spread wide.

Think think think. What now?

'I didn't want to have to do this,' she said. 'But you should know that I've got a . . . *hedgehog.*' She whipped him out of her pocket. 'And I'm not afraid to use him. Get back or he'll . . . do something.'

'Any time, Hoggins,' she whispered, as Bron's maddened red eyes drew closer.

CHAPTER 22

Bron was poised to leap when the whip-crack voice of the Nocturne cut the air.

'Bronagh, a moment.' The Nocturne raised a bandaged hand to halt the angry Pooka. 'I'll attend to this.'

Bron, uncertain, stepped aside as the Nocturne limped through the long grass and stood before Emily, who was still holding the Hog out like a loaded gun. He'd stopped the Nocturne herself dead in her tracks once before. Surely that meant something? Surely her mum had sent him along for a secret magical reason? The Hog himself was squirming to turn around and catch her eye.

'Oh child, you don't understand anything, do you?' The

Nocturne's voice was almost sympathetic. Her half-smile twisted out from under the porcelain blankness. The Hog's little face was all scrunched up and, in so far as a hedgehog could be said to look sad, he did. He shook his head then hung it low.

'What?' She was talking to both the Hog and the Nocturne, but only one of them answered.

'*All* you have is a hedgehog.' The Nocturne's half-grin broadened, and with it came a glimpse of the beauty that music had restored.

The Nocturne continued talking, but she was looking directly at the Hog, not at Emily.

'You can do nothing. No rules have been broken, no ancient law crossed. All I seek to do is restore the balance of the world and no oaths are broken to do so.' A knife of a smile. 'You have no power over me. Now get out of my way.'

She lashed out then, fast as a striking snake, and smacked Emily's hands where they clutched the Hog. Despite the Nocturne's depleted state, it was still like getting whacked by a hammer, the gnarled fingers and nails like wood and iron. Emily yelled with sudden pain and the little brown shape of Hoggins flew so far he sailed out of sight into the bushes with a squeak and a crash.

'No! My Hoggins!'

Anger sang through Emily, lighting her bones on fire.

She reached inside herself for the best thing to channel that anger. She grabbed on to fur and teeth and claws and hauled them over herself, her rage stretching them to a size to fit the vastness of her fury, her teeth bursting into a mouthful of fangs to better show her need for revenge.

She curved forwards to the ground, her arms now thick legs with wicked claws at the tips, ridged with muscle and covered with a fine grey fur like morning fog. She shook out her shoulders and her long back rippled all the way down to her furiously lashing tail. She was not a podgy, scared terrier this time; she was a large and furious hound with a mouthful of sharp teeth. The vibration of a swarm of bees filled her chest and head; she was growling, a guttural buzzing noise that filled the air between her and this hated enemy. She let the growl build all the way up in her throat, threw back her head and let out a bone-chilling howl.

The Nocturne's half-face changed from a vicious look of triumph to one of pale worry, both sides equally blank and white. She took a step back. Drool dripped from Emily's jaws as she gnashed them together. She tried to shout 'You hurt my Hoggins' but all that came out was an avalanche of roaring, snarling barking. Judging from the look on the Nocturne's face, the message got through anyway.

Emily braced herself to spring. She wasn't thinking very

clearly, but the oldest part of her brain, the part that had sharp, sharp teeth, was telling her the throat was the softest bit. She drew up all the power in her legs, formed herself into a spring and then . . . was slammed sideways as a black furry weight cannonballed into her, and started lashing out with claws and teeth. A familiar scent filled her nose – it was Bron.

Normal Emily would have scarpered, but hound Emily was wild and strong and eager for a challenge. She growled and clawed and caught a mouthful of fur to bite down on. There was a surprised yelp, then she was up and facing the big black red-eyed doom of Bron as they circled each other, snarling. She was big, bigger than Emily, but not by much, not compared to Mammy Espeth's form. Emily's new shape was sleek, muscled and fast, and her jaws were strong. If she could stay out from under Bron's feet then . . . Bron darted in and they clashed, the clack of their teeth hitting each other like branches cracking in a storm. White light filled her head at the force of it, then another whipping pass and turn, faster and faster, roaring and snarling and tumbling, as they went for each other, out for blood.

The world shrank down to the tiny universe that was their struggle, all growling and slashing and panting, until that was all there was of her. As long as she kept moving, she was ahead, but Bron had fought a hundred times before, and knew how to use her weight and strength.

Emily was forced down then under Bron and she couldn't get up. There were jaws at her neck, not ripping because her fur was too thick, but biting and holding, making it hard to breathe when it was already hard to breathe. She was starting to see spots and colours and her back legs and tail thrashed on the ground but couldn't break her free.

She couldn't win, but she couldn't afford to lose – it was too important. She thought of Mammy fighting the Bear, and had a really stupid idea. She did it before common sense could talk her out of it. She rippled back into human form, and her less furry self fell out from the jaws that gripped her. Now she lay under a snarling black beast confused as to why anybody would be so stupid as to change back into a squishy human during a dog fight. Bron's awful snarling muzzle of fangs was inches away from Emily's face, and she didn't have her thick pelt to protect her anymore. Bron reared back to strike and Emily fought off the pain and the fear. She pulled back her arm and, putting all that was left of her hedgehog-abuse rage into it, punched Bron on the end of her sensitive dog nose as hard as ever she could.

'Boop!' she yelled, and Bron gave a whimpering howl, rolling off her into a bed of moonflowers, clutching at her nose with her paws.

Emily staggered to her feet. She hadn't got away unscathed herself. Her neck and shoulder were screaming with pain, and she could feel a thick and sticky wetness running down her arm that might just be blood. The sickening nausea that came after a change was flooding through her too. The fight might have gone on for an hour but it must have been less than a minute. She was still gasping for breath when an awful noise shredded the air. It was like the universe coming off its rails, a discordant screeching that she felt as much as heard. Suppressing a very strong urge to do otherwise, she ran straight towards it, and burst through a small hawthorn coppice to see something terrible.

The Nocturne must have totally ignored the dog fight and gone straight for the Hole. She was standing in front of it, in between the pillars and deep in the shadow of the arched portico of the church above. Her head was tilted, listening to sounds that no one else could hear, and her hands were plunged deep into the golden glimmer of the outer edge of the Hole. The throbbing dread-noise was coming from it as it strained against reality. It ran and foamed golden over the Nocturne's hands, rippling and warping as she twisted her fingers into distorted positions. The Hole gave off plumes of golden sparks, fizzing and crackling like the most terrifying popping candy in the world. The sparks tumbled into the void at the centre of the Hole, whirling then vanishing, like water gurgling down the biggest drain ever. Hopefully the 'going down the plughole' look wasn't a bad omen for the future of, well, everything.

Emily staggered forwards, wondering what happened if you rugby-tackled a demigod.

'Oi, Milpo, get off that! Or I'll, erm . . .' Her brain was grinding as she struggled to think. Everything ached from the fight and she couldn't catch her breath. 'Just pack it in, right!'

Great. That'll do it. She needed to be more annoying.

'How did it feel when that bell landed on your head?'

The Nocturne paused. Her shoulders stiffened and she turned to face Emily, still leaving one hand in the globs of light at the edge of the spasming Hole.

'Pathetic creature.' Her smile was vicious. 'Look at the desolation of your hopes. Look at my victory. What did you possibly think you could achieve here?'

As she spoke, a leather-clad fury loomed out of the shadows and stepped in between the Nocturne and Emily. Bron had flicked back to human form, and was holding her bashed-up nose, and glaring straight at Emily with murder in her red eyes. Emily was too exhausted to change again, and Bron was stronger than her anyway. The fight was lost. So it was confusing for both Bron and the Nocturne when Emily looked past them at the Hole, and grinned.

'Oh, nothing,' she smiled wide and broad, despite the throb from her worryingly damp shoulder, 'other than keeping you occupied until this happened.'

The Nocturne snarled and turned back to the Hole. The edge flared molten gold at the point the Nocturne's hand gripped it, but there was a shadow in the very centre of the Hole now. A darkness rushing towards them in the golden eddies of the absence. The Nocturne stepped back, her hand reappearing from wherever it had been. The shape swirled and grew vast and then in a blink was an inkblot, then a shadow the height of a man, until from the storm of time itself stepped . . .

A highly suspicious-looking Irishman in a battered black tweed suit with a flat cap pulled low over his black hair, and a roll-up sticking out one side of his mouth. It was Uncle Pat, and he was carrying a great big armful of rolled-up paper.

'Howayiz, missus? Interrupting am I?'

He took another look at who he was talking to and blanched. He grabbed at his cap. 'Ye all seem fierce busy. I'll leave yez to it.'

Bron snarled, and the Nocturne came for him, hands extended into claws, but Pat was suddenly shoved out of the way from behind and stumbled forwards, scrolls of paper tumbling to the ground around him. Behind him, looming in the Hole as shadows, then erupting like bowling balls, came more Pooka. First cousin Artie (identifiable by the pronounced horsey teeth), then another face, family resemblance obvious by the shiftiness, then another and another. They flooded out of the Hole, each of them weighed down with a heavy armful, each of them having the same experience as Pat – a sudden encounter with a terrifying Older Power causing them to back-pedal, then a new arrival or three from behind pushing them forward into a near collision. The Nocturne was jostled, pushed back and eventually disappeared behind a wall of Pooka all pushing and bumping into each other, staggering into flower beds, and cursing. Bron gaped in horror. First ten, then twenty, and then the whole clan were there.

Emily's dad had once said the collective noun for Pooka was 'an argument', and he had surely been right. There was a sea of them, the whole clan bickering and holding things and shouting at each other.

Every single one of the Pooka was carrying something: from framed pictures to metal sculptures of horses' heads to wall hangings. Emily grinned. It was every single piece of art from her house, everything her mum had ever sculpted, painted, welded or chipped into life, all pried off the wall and dragged through the Hole. Just like she'd asked Mammy to do in the back room of the Coach and Horses, when she'd told her the two final places the Hole would stop at, and talked her into going out one and back in the other and convincing the Pooka they'd be staging an outrageously audacious art heist in between.

One of the Pooka, a younger woman, was holding the Abbits, the spinning black glass mobile from Emily's bedroom wall. Standing next to her was a young Pooka girl holding a very comforting-looking cuddly crocodile.

'Oi, that's my Feesh!' shouted Emily, but her voice was lost in the hubbub.

In the thickness of the crowd, Emily caught a glimpse of a black fur coat and a shock of white hair, and then her definitely-not-nan, Mammy, was there.

'You smell of hound.' She gave a small approving nod. 'It all went grand, so. Tight getting back in, mind. Good job there's a time lag.'

She squeezed Emily's non-bleeding shoulder, and the warmth from it coursed into her.

The comfort didn't last long. A voice echoed across the crowd, audible even above the Pooka din.

'Emily Featherhaugh, on my sainted Aunt Aoife's life, but you are in so much trouble.'

Mammy winced.

'There was one small problem, y'know.'

They hadn't just stolen the art. They'd stolen her mum too.

OH. EM. GEE.

CHAPTER 23

Her mum was storming towards her, tummy bulging, bad pennies necklace swaying and glinting in the witchlight. Her eyes were wild with anger. Maeve halted in front of Emily, pointed her index finger like a loaded pistol and set to.

'*Popping out for a run*, she says. Knows she's grounded she does. Already in fierce trouble business, and *look* where she is.' She fired the finger under Emily's nose and Emily's stomach curdled. '*Then*, already in trouble beyond mortal ken, she sends *that* woman to my house.'

Here her mum briefly pointed the finger gun at Mammy, before bringing it back to its original target. 'An' a bunch of eejits convinced they were being away off on a priceless art heist!'

Emily peered over Maeve's shoulder. Where had the Nocturne gone? Where was the Bear? Was Tarkus okay?

'Mum, not only have I got like the most incredible excuse for all this, but we've kinda got a situation here.'

Maeve narrowed her eyes, but before she could answer a terrible sound split the air.

It started as the notes of a distant police siren, rising and falling, then growing in intensity and volume, until it became teeth-clenching, eye-squinting, hands-over-ears loud. It filled the gardens and a gap appeared in the crowd as the furthest Pooka tumbled like dominoes, clutching their ears. The wave had rippled in from over at the green-house side of the piazza. At the centre of it, the Nocturne was howling, head thrown back like an opera singer, and jaw opened wider than any human's could have gone. She looked like a snake about to swallow a guinea pig, and sounded like a foghorn on the *Titanic*. She overwhelmed all other noise and stillness rippled out from her as the Pooka tumbled.

Bron was standing behind her, looking desperately awkward for once. Behind her, the Bear was wobbling unsteadily, eyes still rolling, but out from under the spell. Emily's heart raced as she searched for Tarkus, until his hand gripped her elbow as he wormed through those left standing. He was covered in mud and had a giant bruise developing on one side of his face, but all of his arms and legs were there, so she wasn't too worried. They had time to share only a look and a grim nod, before the Nocturne stopped screaming. All eyes were on the Older Power.

'You ridiculous animals.' She wasn't speaking in much more than a husky whisper, but her words rang in everybody's ears. A distant thrum of darkly chorded music ran under them.

'Was this your plan? Overwhelm me with idiots?'

There was a grizzly mutter from the remaining Pooka, which dropped away sharply as she glared at them.

Mammy Espeth growled, her thin shoulders tensed under her vast coat, as her shadow shifted on the floor beneath her.

'Will you really test yourself against me, Espeth Shelagh Lugh Conol?' The Nocturne pointed at Mammy. 'With your family around you? Run now, for I will strike all of you down. You know I can.'

Seeing Pat lurking not far from her, Emily reached over and grabbed one of the scrolls of paper he was holding. He winked at her, but she was too sick with fear to wink back.

She held the scroll to her chest, fist clenched so tight it hurt, and stepped past Mammy to face the Nocturne.

'Why, oh why, do you have to be such a total git?'

Behind her, her mum and Mammy took a position at

each of her shoulders, and Tarkus stood to the side, the Hole at their back. The rest of the Pooka stood in a semi-circle around her too, but far back enough to have plausible deniability of being on her side if it all went wrong. The Nocturne sneered as they faced her, and the Bear loomed at her side, although Bron wavered further back.

'You think three generations of one-trick ponies have the power to stop me?' Her blue eyes shone with a cold light. 'We are moments from the end of all of this and the start of my new reign. Then all debts will be settled.'

'Yeah,' said Emily. 'Debts are about to be settled, you hog-whacker.'

She unrolled the scroll of paper. On it was one of the sequence of horse sketches her mum had done in strokes of black ink. The horse, repeated three times in different parts of its stride, running across the thick white paper.

'Please work,' she said quietly to herself. Then, aloud, 'Come to me, please. Come to me as I came to you.' Then, just in case it would help, she leant close and whispered. 'My mum's here too.'

The Nocturne hissed, but Emily didn't look up, just kept her gaze fixed on the horses. For an infinity, nothing happened. Her hands tightened into white-knuckled fists and scrunched the paper where she was holding it. It made the horses look like they were moving in the moonlight, and then she saw that they *were*. Their ink-slashed manes were blowing in the wind, and their legs were no longer captive mid-stride, but falling and hitting the sketched-in ground with a drumming impact that throbbed through the paper.

The horses were running now, off one edge of the paper and back on the other. They ran so fast that soon they blurred into just one horse. The black of the ink thickened and then the horse had a rider. It was clear the rider was a woman, despite her only being sketched in simple lines. The paper became heavier and heavier until it tore itself from her hands and fell to the grassy floor where it curled and bucked, wracked by a great wind no one else could feel.

All around them, the piles of art that had been brought through by the Pooka were coming to life. The sculptures twitched and twisted and the paintings whirled into kalei-doscopes. The Abbits were in there, ears and legs spinning faster and faster in a black blur. Many of the artworks were hovering off the ground, and they started a low and lazy spin, sailing off and out from the grips of the Pooka, and began to orbit the crowd. The art twisted and writhed as it circled them, speeding faster and faster, rising up higher and higher, a fairground spinner gathering speed. The Nocturne's face twisted in a terrible, bloodless snarl.

The paper scroll of horses lay on the floor at the centre of the circle, dark as an open trapdoor. The sound of hoof-beats grew and grew, and rose into thunder, and then, with a flash of black light, a life-size horse and rider burst from the paper and into the world. The spinning art around them all crashed to the floor at once.

The horse was part ink and part real, shimmering and strange, but completely alive. It bucked and reared furiously, until the rider laid a gentle hand on its neck and settled it. She was woman-shaped but slicked with colours, the whole of a rainbow sliding over her like oil on water. The rider dismounted lightly and Emily took a halting step forwards, and found her mum had too. The colours fell from the rider like a cloak dropping to the floor. It was Art returned, and veiled no longer.

Her face was a mix of both of her sisters': long nose, tanned skin and eyes that were the stippled colours of every painting ever. There was none of the bone-thin distress or terrible shifting voids Emily had seen before. The puckering of a scar tugged at the corner of her mouth, and thick silvered marks scored up her face and into her hair, but she stood tall now, and the burning, sick heat of before was gone. Her glittering multicoloured eyes took in Emily and her mum, and she smiled. Emily glanced at her mum, and saw eyes full of tears and a rumpled smile. It felt too private a moment to watch, and Emily was about to turn away when Art beat her to it.

Art turned around, all smiles vanished. She stood in grim, fixed silence, raised one hand and pointed straight at the Nocturne. She was standing between the Nocturne and the Hole and her eyes were a storm. A spectrum of light washed out over the gardens, as all other light and colour folded into her. Her shadow grew and pulsed and she was taller than before. Around her, the scattered art on the floor began to twist and move again. Emily was glad it wasn't her she was pointing at.

The Nocturne returned her stare, then her sapphire glance dipped away, her hood covered her face, and her shoulders shook. The Bear and Bron looked on in fear. Emily's heart leapt with joy; they had her on the run. Then from beneath the Nocturne's hood and mask came the most awful noise, a cacophony of broken glass and babies crying. The Nocturne was laughing.

'I applaud your sense of drama, sister, but what exactly do you think this is going to do?' Her voice was warm with good humour.

Emily looked desperately between them. The Nocturne stood confidently, and Art still glowed but her face was fraught. Her accusing finger drifted downwards.

'She's going to fix you and your bloomin' Hole, that's what!' Emily yelled.

'Art will not stand in my way, will you sister? Not after last time.'

The Nocturne took a step forwards, and Art wavered then took a step back. Her light dimmed and some of the floating objects crashed to the floor.

'I thought not.'

'Whoa! No, wait, you can't let her bully you,' Emily said and rushed to Art's side, but Art would not look at her.

'Oh, did you want a grand finale? A magical duel where the evil witch is defeated, perhaps?' The Nocturne's porcelain mask was as impassive as her voice.

That had kinda been exactly what Emily was hoping for, but she wasn't going to admit it.

'There is nothing you, or she, can do. I won this battle before it started.' The Nocturne grinned, and it was a glinting sickle blade in her half-face. 'You are dead but still walking.'

'Nobody's dying here apart from ye, yer wagon.'

It was Maeve, sounding cold and deadly, and angrier than Emily had ever heard her. She had stepped up to stand alongside Art and Emily and she held out the necklace of bad pennies which gleamed silver in the witchlight.

'I've got yer duel right here. Do ye fancy another dose of these?'

The last time the Nocturne had got up close with the cursed bad pennies (after Emily had tipped them all over her) the dose of bad luck had wiped her out of existence with a giant bell landing on her. Right here and now, she didn't even flinch.

'Ah, the Judas silver. It is fitting that what once

destroyed me now paves my way to victory.'

'What are ye blethering about? No more warnings, ye get out of here, or I'll ruin ye.'

'I told you. I've already won. In fact, I won as you thought you defeated me a year ago. Did you not notice one of your nasty little coins was gone?'

Maeve cursed and glared at the necklace she was holding. There had been one missing after all!

'Once a coin of ill-fortune sprang from me into the workings of the clock, then the first note of my symphony of destruction was played.'

The Nocturne was regal as she spoke.

'What you call the Hole is a penny-sized break in the Great Working, a discord in the rhythm that has played my tune.'

She waved her bandaged hands in the air, conducting an invisible orchestra.

'Even as you have played out your little farce of resurrection, my last notes have been played, and only the coda remains.'

She gestured behind them. 'Look, sister. It's too late. Your world fades to diminuendo and silence, and I am free.'

Emily looked behind her and realized Tarkus had been right. There was something she didn't know she didn't know.

Behind them, unnoticed in the confrontation, the Hole

had started to go horribly wrong. Where before it had been a circle, now it bulged and shifted, a twisting distortion that wobbled round and round as it spun out of shape, a pot gone wonky on a potter's wheel. It was throbbing with light, not the lean gold of before but a sickly yellow and a jaundiced green. It was curdled and lumpen and getting worse. As they watched, it started to spin faster and grow bigger, fragments of light leeching out from it, cracks in the very fabric of the Midnight Hour.

'That's never good,' said Pat.

CHAPTER 24

The Nocturne wasn't smiling now, and her voice rang louder in every ear.

'This *is* the grand finale and there is nothing you can do. I have already torn asunder the weak point in the Great Working.'

The Hole's radiance played gold and shadows on her face as she spoke. 'Now the Hole rips open, the magic pours out under my control and I shall wield it in the Daylight realm.'

There were groans of fear from the Pooka. Art clutched a hand to her mouth in silent horror, and Maeve stood white-knuckled, not sure what to punch. Emily's stomach curdled and she thought she might throw up.

The Nocturne walked towards the Hole now. Maeve hefted the coins but the Bear's vast bulk limped at the Nocturne's side as a living shield, and it was too late.

'I am no monster. Those who kneel to me will be welcome to share in my new world of freedom, but this prison is done.' She was smiling as if on her way to buy ice cream at the beach.

'No, you can't!' shouted Emily and lunged after her, only to find a steely grip on her wrist holding her back. It was her mum, who shook her head with a bitter frown on her face. Ahead of them, the Nocturne stepped into the heaving maelstrom of the Hole. She did not look back once. Her silhouette flickered against the terrible light then was gone out into the world, followed by the hulking shadow of the Bear.

Bron was just behind them. She gave one anguished look back at Mammy, who held out an open hand. Bron hovered for an awful moment, then her face crumpled and she ran into the light after the Nocturne. Mammy sighed and rubbed a hand over her face.

Another noise filled the air now, the whistling roar of a window being opened in a speeding car. A stiff gust of wind jolted Emily where she was standing, and all the pieces of canvas and parchment were caught by it and flapped towards the Hole. The Hole pulsed and throbbed, and had grown bigger again. The faint water-down-the-drain look of the earlier sparks had become a full-on whirlpool with a lava glow. There was a great movement and whistling in the air, and the leaves on all the trees and bushes were in ferment. The wind howled and became visible, glinting with the emerald glow of sorcery as it surged into the widening gap. Colour pulsed from it and flaming light roared from the edges of the Hole. The moon itself flickered and Emily saw a cloud shift slightly in a sky that hadn't changed since 1859.

The Nocturne had been right. The Hole was ripping the world open and all the magic was being sucked out behind her. This was the end of the Midnight Hour.

'We've got to do something!' Emily yelled, as much to herself as anyone else. She just didn't know what. She ran to Art and grabbed her arm. The Older Power was still feather-light despite her recovery.

'Help us. You built it, you must be able to fix it.'

The scars on Art's face were tugged white by fear, but she nodded once in a tiny movement. She braced herself against the howling magical wind and held her hands out together before her. Her unnaturally long fingers allowed her to make almost a perfect circle shape with them. Her eyes flickered with rainbow light, and her hands began to pulse with the sickened gold glow of the Hole. She went rigid with sudden strain, and her hands began to bleed light as she attempted to weave together what the Nocturne had unravelled.

Another hand slipped into Emily's. It was her mum, her face strained and pale.

'I don't think she's strong enough. She's only just come back and ...'

Her mum was right. Art was visibly shrinking from the towering height she'd grown to earlier. The silver tracery of scars pulled tight over her face as she strained. She was impossibly fragile and couldn't last and then ... the Library was there. She winked into being from a cloud of ink and stepped hesitantly towards Art, her face twisted by worry. Art flinched back as she saw her. The Library said nothing, just held her hand out to Art. Emily held her breath and after an endless moment, Art nodded.

The Library stepped behind her, held her arms out as if to hug her, then gently placed her hands over her sister's, joining and strengthening the circle. Where they touched the colours glowed through both of them, and a beam of light joined them to the Hole. Art's eyes glowed with the rainbow renewed and the Hole shook and shrank just a little. Emily's heart leapt. The two of them, together, could do it.

Then Art's face distorted with the silent scream Emily had previously seen carved in stone, and her hands sprang apart. The light left her and she collapsed. The Library gave an anguished cry, matched by Maeve, who ran forwards with Emily. The Library was cradling her motionless sister, shielding her from the storm with her own body as they reached them.

'It was too much. Too much. I should have kept her safe.'

'It's not your fault!' shouted Emily. 'Please, can you still close it? We'll look after her.'

The Library wept blackened tears.

'The original spell took both of us. I cannot do it without her. We are lost.'

'NO!' shouted Emily. 'Just no bloomin' way. Not now.'

She stared around at everything, at her newly discovered extended family, at her best friend, and at the Hole about to destroy all of their lives, and desperately tried to think of a plan.

'We have to stop it!' Tarkus yelled at her, barely audible over the roar.

'I'm working on it!'

The Hole flared with volcanic light. It had expanded to fill the space between the pillars, and the double oaken doors of the church were perfectly framed through it. They heaved with the pressure of the gale building against them. The wind ripped off clumps of sable moonflowers and whipped them round in the air like ungainly birds, even as that very air bruised and darkened with the weight of magic pouring through where the Nocturne had walked out.

A firework went off in her head. *Doors. Birds. Out.*

She grabbed Tarkus and yelled straight down his ear. 'It's a bird!'

'What?!' he shouted back, rocked by the wind.

'It's a blooming bird! You can close it.'

'Did you hit your head? What's a bird?'

'That!' She pointed at the Hole. 'It's an egret! So you can use the Master Key on it!'

'EGRESS! It's an egress!' Even in this time of utter disaster he still managed to look annoyed.

'EXACTLY! Something one goes *out of*. Are you in charge of them or what?'

Tarkus became completely still, apart from his eyes which swirled with flame while he thought. He nodded, first slowly, then faster.

'It might just work. It's part of the original spell.' He was already scrabbling at his jacket and produced the glowing key on its chain. It looked terribly small in the face of the ever-growing doom portal. She gripped his arm.

'I'm guessing neither of us has a better idea?' she said.

He shook his head. As one they strode forwards, her mum yelling something behind them that was blown away on the wind. Emily wasn't sure if they could even get to the Hole. The wind was screaming into it and lashing everything in front of it to pieces. They had to drop to their knees and crawl, occasionally ducking to avoid flying sculpture and branches. She struggled forward, barely able to breathe and half blind, to the malformed edge that throbbed with furnace light.

Tarkus grasped the key and she grasped his hand so they held it together. He shouted the incantation over the wind.

'Moon's light, preserve the night. This door's ward, by the Accord, I bid thee close!'

The key lit up with the electric green light of the Great Working itself and trebled in size. Together, as one, they plunged it into the pulsing border of the Hole between worlds. Emily had half expected to be whipped into the tunnel, but instead as they jammed the key into the swirl of colour, it slid into it like a lock and held firm in mid-air. The colour of the Hole around the key changed back to its original copper glow, but the gale of magic didn't falter.

'We need to turn it widdershins,' yelled Tarkus.

'What?'

'Anticlockwise,' he somehow managed to tut while shouting. She glared at him, but decided to save the dressing down until after the apocalypse. Together they leant into the wind and turned the key as hard as they could. Or tried to. It wouldn't budge.

The energy spilling from the Hole was fierce. Emily was half blinded by the light and searing pains were scorching through her hands. Tarkus winced next to her but they both held on desperately as they tried to turn the key again. Still nothing.

'It's not working!' Tarkus had to duck as a small rhododendron bush was blown over his head. 'It must be the damage to the spell.'

'No! We've got to try harder. We just need . . . *something*.'

Emily reached inside herself, groping for dog strength, anything, and found a remaining squiggle of quicksilver luck. She seized it, and then on instinct reached out to see if there was more. If she pushed her luck then maybe she . . . suddenly there was more, not a squiggle but a wellspring, a potent force she recognized. Mammy. Mammy was reaching into her own reservoir of luck and pushing it on to Emily. Not a theft, but a gift. She wrapped herself and the key in it, but it still wasn't enough. She sobbed as the clouds above her shifted across the moon, blotting the light for the first time in centuries.

A voice roared behind her, audible over the storm. Mammy yelling at the clan.

'Ye will all give what luck ye have. I know ye've got it tucked away, ye grasping lot!'

Emily shot a look over her shoulder and saw Mammy magnificently raging, white hair lashed by the storm, and giving the evil eye to the whole clan.

'She is clan now! She's turned hound, tricked ye all here, and stood off the worst power in the land with nothing but cheek and teeth.'

Emily could hear something else too. Not through her ears but through the Pooka pulse of blood and luck she was connected to now – the clan chorus.

She's got a point, there, y'know. Had us all goin' on like pups.

Passed the test sure enough. Grand, so.

From all around, red gleaming eyes stared at Mammy. 'She is yer blood, and by rowan and silver, ye will aid her, or ye'll get my teeth in yer ars—'

She was drowned out by a rising baying howl – it came first from a familiar voice, Pat, then a chorus of other voices joined in as the Pooka howled as one. Her mum's clear voice rose to join them and, head thrown back, Mammy did too. The midnight howl of the Pooka clan united, as clean and silver-sharp as church bells. Emily reached for her luck again and now it wasn't a well but a river, a torrent, a flood she could barely handle. She took the tidal wave of quicksilver from them all inside herself, and prayed it would be enough. She gripped hard on to Tarkus's hand and together they tried again. The clan howled above the storm and she squeezed every single drop of gleaming mercury luck on to their hands, the key, the lock; on to this one moment in time that *had* to turn out okay.

The key bucked and jangled with a sudden electricity and began to turn, and the Hole flickered. They both leant in to give it everything, teeth bared with the effort. She felt herself become a channel for the clan's combined luck, a quicksilver river, an inescapable natural force that could eat away at mountains. With the weight of her whole family's strength behind her hand, the key turned all the way round. The Hole folded in on itself, and flickered out of existence with a gout of golden light and an escaped-balloon raspberry noise. The wind stopped, the clouds cleared, and pale silver moonlight blessed the gardens once more. Emily fell over in a heap with Tarkus.

She lay there on the damp moss of the church porch, her hand still gripped with Tarkus's on the key. Neither of them spoke although there was a lot of Irish whooping in the background. After a while, Emily noticed a familiar snuffling form with a damp nose pressed to her leg. She held her hand out and a four-footed, warm-bellied weight scuttled up and filled it.

'That, Hog, was a close one.' She stroked his nose. 'I was never worried, obvs.'

CHAPTER 25

As the gardens became quiet and still, and the half-deafened Pooka clan, two battered demigods, one very bruised ghûl, and a thankfully unflattened hedgepig all took a breath, a black shape arced out of the sky at the speed of a rocket. It whistled into the gardens, skimming the heads of the crowd of Pooka, effected a screeching skid of a landing, then separated into two black shapes, as the tensed figure riding the flying bike hurled himself off into a forward roll and sprang to his feet, drawing a sword as he landed. The sword burst into flames, illuminating the face of Emily's dad.

'Oh,' he said. 'Is it all over?'

Her mum patted at her dungarees, which were somewhat damper than previously.

'Erm no, it's just starting. This baby's coming.'

'Oh, er, ah,' said her dad, turning from right to left, shedding little fireballs from his sword as he did.

'Alan, would ye turn the flippin' sword off before ye set someone on fire, and come and give me a hand.'

'We need to get to hospital,' he said.

'I'm not going through a time door while I'm giving birth. Anything could happen. Double birthdays and all sorts.'

The Library spoke from where she knelt with her sister cradled against her.

'I have read every book on obstetrics ever written.'

Maeve shied away.

'Up until 1859, ye have! That doesn't even cover hand washing!'

'Ah for pity's sake. Off with ye.' Mammy shouldered in and flapped her hands at the Library as if shooing away a nosy cat. She put a gentle hand on Maeve's arm.

'Come away here and I'll get ye sorted. I've attended more of these than I can count.' She turned and shouted. 'Patrick, I want somewhere found with blankets and a bed and hot water, and I want it all yesterday, or ye'll be regretting it.'

'Yes, Mammy. Right away, Mammy,' Pat yelled as he sprinted off, hanging on to his cap as he ran.

'How are ye off fer gin?' Mammy asked Maeve, waving a small flask she'd pulled from her pocket.

'I'm giving birth, not going on a pub crawl and . . . don't think yer lighting that filthy thing by me!' she shrieked as Mammy pulled her pipe out instead.

They headed after Pat, still bickering, but arm in arm, with Emily's dad trailing behind, sword still held uncertainly in hand, like an extinguished sparkler. Emily smiled.

Behind her, now the fireworks were over, the Pooka were doing that very casual sidling walk they had all perfected at an early age. They used this as a way of leaving places quietly when legally dubious events had occurred, particularly if people with wide-ranging legal powers had just turned up. Emily scowled at a small figure that hadn't quite perfected the stealth-sidle yet.

'Oi, short and furry! Don't think you're walking off with my blooming Feesh either!' She beckoned meaningfully. 'Hand over the crocodile and be about your business.'

The little Pooka girl's face twisted with anger and she shook her head, but the young woman with her whispered in her ear, and gave her a shove until she marched over and held it out to Emily. Emily reached to take it, and the little Pooka girl's eyes welled up, and her face shifted and became furry until she was literally doing puppy eyes. Her little paws gripped on to the green verdant fur of the Feesh and wouldn't let go.

Emily looked down and bit her lip.

'Y'know, it'd probably be a heart-warming thing for me to let you keep this.' She narrowed her eyes. 'But he's my Feesh, so there's not a chance.'

She yanked him out of the Pooka kid's hands and gripped him tightly. The little girl hissed, growled, turned into a snarling miniature hound, and nipped Emily in the ankle before running off howling.

'You are an inspiration for us all,' said Tarkus, limping over as she was hopping around trying to rub her ankle.

'Yeah, well, never trust a Pooka. I told Mammy to keep them out of my bedroom!'

'I presume you're aware you're bleeding?' He pointed at her shoulder.

'I presume you're aware it looks like someone stood on your head?'

'That is exactly what happened, in fact.' He rubbed tenderly at the swollen side of his face. 'Well, we appear to have saved the world again.'

'And without the help you should have had.' It was the Library, walking beside a now-upright Art with an arm wrapped around her for support. 'We owe you a debt, and I owe you an apology.'

Tarkus stiffened, but then gave a sweeping bow. 'Never, Great Lady. Family means all to my people. I understand.' He winced on the way back up, but it was still pretty smooth, Emily thought.

'Ladies, gotta ask . . . what happened to *her*?' Emily didn't need to say a name.

'We cannot survive outside, there is not enough magic for us to exist,' said the Library.

Art gestured at her sister, her fingers flickering too fast to follow. The Library nodded and spoke for her.

'Yet her flame still burns. We would know if she were no more.'

'I cannot say I am thankful to hear that, your family or not,' said Tarkus. Emily looked at him in shock, but he pressed on. 'It's just, it was *so* close. It's been so close both times.' He faltered, rubbed at his swollen brow. 'She's not going to stop trying, is she? So what happens to everybody when we get it wrong?'

Nobody spoke. Art shook her head slowly, her scars rippling as she frowned.

'Well then,' said Tarkus. 'We will bid you goodnight. We need to go and get patched up. I think I spotted healing herbs in the corner.'

As they limped away, the sisters first faded then disappeared.

'Oh, wait!' shouted Emily but it was too late, they were gone.

'What?' said Tarkus.

'I was trying to tell her not to forget her horse,' said

Emily. Ahead of them, the half-ink, half-real, all horse that Art had ridden in on was still standing in the middle of the gardens, chewing contentedly on an abandoned watercolour.

Five minutes later, they were picking their way through the compress cauliflower patch, with a large hand-drawn horse trotting behind them. Suddenly, a figure with a very pointy hat loomed out of the dark.

'Whoa, you made me jum— Oh! It's you. Hello?' said Emily.

Under the shadow of the pointy hat was a hooked nose, a bristly chin and seriously suspect dentistry, all attached to a green-tinged face. It was the very-probably-not-a-witch, Ma Shipton, from the Night Market.

'I believe you made a binding promise to come for tea. I'm here to take you.' Her voice was gravelly and determined.

'Errm,' said Emily.

'Now, madame, this is not the time,' said Tarkus in his most officious of voices.

The probably-just-a-misunderstood-cat-rescuer's eyes flashed with a flicker of violet light.

'This was a promise given within the Night Market.'

'Oh.' Tarkus turned to Emily in horror. 'What did I tell you about the Night Market rules?! You'll have to go. I'll try and send help as soon as I can.'

'*What?*'

'You promised, and now you must come to tea. I've

been looking forward to it all week.' Ma Shipton's smile was full of teeth that were frankly ominous.

'Now hang on—' began Emily but, before she'd finished, the maybe-a-botanist's fingernails were wreathed in a purple energy, there was a *Kerzapp!* noise and she was swallowed up in billowing purple smoke as the world vanished.

'I've got to say, Mrs S, these are astonishingly good cakes,' Emily said, although it came out mangled due to the amount of the aforementioned cake in her face.

'Do you really think so?' said Ma Shipton from her armchair by the fire in the snug little parlour. She smiled her alarming smile which, Emily was coming to realize, was probably caused by her very sweet tooth.

'Yeah, they're great. I'm totally an expert too.' Emily paused to shove away the big black purring cat face that had just stuffed itself under her chin. 'No, Grimalkin, we've talked about this.' The cat curled back down into her blanket-draped lap, which he had retreated to after a prickly discussion with the Hog. The victor of that debate was munching the edge of a scone on the table, and looking very pleased with himself.

'Oh, he's such a silly when people come round. He's beside himself today with all this excitement.'

'Yeah, what are the odds of you living right by Coven

Gardens, eh?'

Emily shifted in the big padded armchair to get her feet closer to the fire, and winced as her shoulder twanged under the fresh new bandage Ma Shipton had wrapped it in.

'Indeed. Fancy it being my door that nice Mr Patrick knocked on for a place for your mother's confinement.'

'Yeah, luck of the Irish that one.' She frowned. 'You don't have any valuables lying around, do you?'

'Nothing in particular. Why do you ask?'

'Oh, no reason. Wait, is that . . . ?'

They both paused to listen. Above the little parlour where they sat eating was the bedroom where they'd taken Emily's mum. There had been a lot of thumping and some absolutely thunderously bad language, but it had all been quiet for a while. Now there was a little cry, and then a full-throated howl in the night.

'Oh, the little chap has got a fine set of lungs, hasn't he?' said Ma Shipton.

'Wow, a brother.' Emily couldn't speak for a moment. 'Hang on, how can you tell it's a boy?'

'Oh, I have my ways, dear.'

Emily looked at the black cat in her lap, the broom by the door, and the victim of oppressive patriarchal ignorance sat opposite her.

'Mrs S, I've got to ask, are you . . .'

'Am I what, dear?'

Ma Shipton's bright eyes were on hers, and she just couldn't do it.

'. . . Are you going to eat that last cake?'

'Bless your heart.' Mrs S beamed and leant over and squeezed her hand and, oddly, her finger. 'No, you have it dear. We must fatten you up.'

'Riiiiiight.'

CODA

And within the world called Daylight, sits a piece of permanent night that wasn't there before. In this place without magic, there is now a sphere of purest midnight so full of it that it gleams like shark's eyes and black pearls.

The sphere is small, big enough only for a demigod and enough magic for her to survive, not thrive, yet it is a foothold in a foreign territory. The first landing of an invasion.

Alone, for now, in midnight isolation, she smiles, for she knows what part of the symphony of destruction plays next.

ACKNOWLEDGEMENTS

From Trindles:

My warmest thanks to Hobbes, Trinders, Wildgeese, Tribe Girls, Stoners*, Zarkoffs, Impropers, and Swaggers, for their endless support, encouragement and kindness. And to Ben, for being a most excellent partner-in-writing-Midnight-crime (and for all the nice dog photos).

*As in Waterstones, of course.

From Read:

A very special thank you to the extended support network of the Books, Improperers, Strat fam, and the Picton Girls. Without whom etc. A grateful doff of the cap to Walt, Lizzie, and Lucy at Inshriach House, for putting up a writer in fine style, and to my Irish swearing consultant, Tony Connolly and his fine family, for letting me steal their name (well, for stealing it, and then telling them after the book came out anyway).

Especially though, to Lau, brightest of buttons, reddest of pens, and best of friends. Without you (and the hedgehog pictures) this insubstantial pageant would simply fade.

From Trindles & Read:

A huge thank you to Elinor, Myers, Jazz, Sarah, Rachel H, and all the chickens at the coop. You're all very good eggs (especially the possibly magical pocket hedgehog of the publishing world, Barry).

A particular thank you to our brilliant editor, Rachel. Always a vital part of the process, but on this particularly difficult ice-skate uphill, your endless kind-hearted support was both invaluable and deeply appreciated. *Bumps fist to chest*

To Hannah Peck, for illustrating our gloriously spooky, and now award-winning, covers.

To all our wonderful readers who have journeyed with us into Midnight once again, and to all the booksellers, teachers, and librarians who helped them find their way through the door as the chimes marked twelve.

THE LAST CHANCE HOTEL by NICKI THORNTON

Seth is the oppressed kitchen boy at the remote Last Chance Hotel, owned by the nasty Bunn family. His only friend is his black cat, Nightshade. But when a strange gathering of magicians arrives for dinner, kindly Dr Thallomius is poisoned by Seth's special dessert. A locked-room murder investigation ensues – and Seth is the main suspect.

The funny thing is, he's innocent . . . can he solve the mystery and clear his name, especially when magic's afoot?

*This mystery is a worthy prizewinner . . .
a jolly, atmospheric mystery.*
THE TIMES

*Hercule Poirot meets Harry Potter in this
mind-bending, magical murder mystery.*
MISS CLEVELAND IS READING

Paperback, ISBN 978-1-911077-67-1, £6.99 • ebook, 978-1-911490-41-8, £6.99

BEETLE BOY by M. G. LEONARD

Darkus can't believe his eyes when a huge insect drops out of the trouser leg of his horrible new neighbour. It's a giant beetle – and it seems to want to communicate.

But how can a boy be friends with a beetle? And what does a beetle have to do with the disappearance of his dad and the arrival of Lucretia Cutter, with her taste for creepy jewellery?

A darkly funny Dahl-esque adventure.
KATHERINE WOODFINE, AUTHOR

A wonderful book, full to the brim with very cool beetles!
THE GUARDIAN

Paperback, ISBN 978-1-910002-70-4, £6.99 • ebook, ISBN 978-1-910002-98-8, £6.99

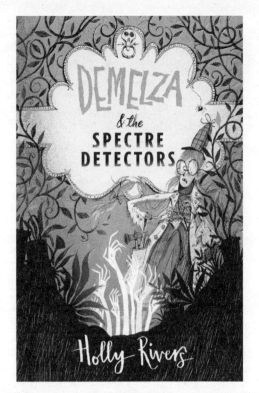

DEMELZA & THE SPECTRE DETECTORS
by HOLLY RIVERS

Demelza loves science – she loves it so much that she stays up late to work on her inventions. But she soon discovers she's also inherited a distinctly unscientific skill: Spectre Detecting.

Like her grandmother, she can summon the ghosts of the dead. When Grandma Maeve is kidnapped, Demelza and her pasty-faced best friend, Percy, must leap into action to solve the deadly mystery . . .

Paperback, ISBN 978-1-912626-03-8, £6.99 • ebook, ISBN 978-1-912626-82-3, £6.99

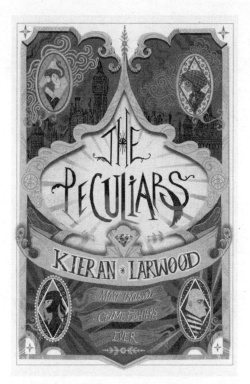

THE PECULIARS by KIERAN LARWOOD

The Peculiars are a band of misfits, trapped in a nightly Victorian sideshow. There's Wolfgirl, Sheba; Sister Moon, who can move at the speed of light; and Monkey Boy, ace climber and human stink bomb. But during the day, in a world of child-snatchers, grave robbers and dastardly doctors, they solve the mysteries no one else cares about – including why London's poorest children are being snatched from the banks of the Thames . . .

> . . . reminiscent of Philip Pullman's immortal Sally Lockhart books.
> THE TIMES

Paperback, ISBN 978-1-911490-21-0, £6.99 • ebook, 978-1-911490-22-7, £6.99